Changing Shifts

Swapping lives, finding love!

In London, widowed pediatrician Georgie is struggling with everyone's sympathy when no one knows her husband was having an affair.

In Edinburgh, pediatrician Clara's dreams of having a family lie in tatters as her ex parades his new love around.

Through a job-swap website, Georgie and Clara impulsively swap cities and hospitals to escape their real lives and embark on new adventures!

But when they arrive at their new destinations, both women find the last thing either wants or expects—romance!

Read Georgie's story in
Fling with Her Hot-Shot Consultant

And Clara's story in
Family for the Children's Doc

Both available now!

Dear Reader,

Scarlet Wilson and I really wanted to write a duet together, with our heroines being complete fish out of water—and we came up with the idea of a job swap. So we plotted together, and my London-based heroine falls for her heroine's best friend in a tiny cottage in the gorgeous countryside outside Edinburgh, while her heroine falls for my heroine's brother smack in the middle of a posh bit of London.

But why would you want to swap jobs and lives with someone in the first place? In Georgie's case, it was to escape her past, and in doing so, she helps Ryan to overcome his past. They start off completely at odds with each other, but, with a bit of canine help, discover that maybe they aren't as bad together as they thought.

Add in men in kilts, the northern lights, a gorgeous beach in Edinburgh, Scottish castles and some very nosy sheep—and I hope you enjoy Georgie and Ryan's journey.

With love,

Kate Hardy

FLING WITH HER HOT-SHOT CONSULTANT

KATE HARDY

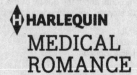

HARLEQUIN

MEDICAL ROMANCE

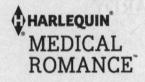

HARLEQUIN®
MEDICAL ROMANCE™

Recycling programs
for this product may
not exist in your area.

ISBN-13: 978-1-335-14949-7

Fling with Her Hot-Shot Consultant

Copyright © 2020 by Pamela Brooks

This edition published by arrangement with Harlequin Books S.A.

For questions and comments about the quality of this book, please contact us at CustomerService@Harlequin.com.

Harlequin Enterprises ULC
22 Adelaide St. West, 40th Floor
Toronto, Ontario M5H 4E3, Canada
www.Harlequin.com

Printed in U.S.A.

Kate Hardy has always loved books, and could read before she went to school. She discovered Harlequin books when she was twelve, and decided that this was what she wanted to do. When she isn't writing, Kate enjoys reading, cinema, ballroom dancing and the gym. You can contact her via her website: katehardy.com.

Books by Kate Hardy

Harlequin Medical Romance

Miracles at Muswell Hill Hospital

Christmas with Her Daredevil Doc
Their Pregnancy Gift

Unlocking the Italian Doc's Heart
Carrying the Single Dad's Baby
Heart Surgeon, Prince...Husband!
A Nurse and a Pup to Heal Him
Mistletoe Proposal on the Children's Ward

Harlequin Romance

A Crown by Christmas

Soldier Prince's Secret Baby Gift

A Diamond in the Snow
Finding Mr. Right in Florence
One Night to Remember

Visit the Author Profile page
at Harlequin.com for more titles.

To Scarlet—always great fun working with you!

PROLOGUE

GEORGIE HAD BEEN secretly haunting the website for a week now.

Job swap.

The idea was that you'd swap your job and your house with a stranger for six months. Various health trusts across the country had signed up to the initiative, so all you had to do was find a match. Someone who did the same job as you; someone who maybe wanted some experience in a different place to enrich their working life.

Was it running away? Or was it just what she needed to give her a fresh start?

It wouldn't be without complications. She'd be letting Joshua down, for a start. Her elder brother was a single dad who relied on her for help with childcare for his daughter Hannah—and Georgie loved her brother and her niece dearly. She didn't want to let them down.

But over the last year London had become

more and more of a prison; and she was oh, so tired of being seen as Poor Georgie, widowed at twenty-nine and being so brave about carrying on. Poor Georgie, who hero husband Charlie had been part of a team of emergency doctors helping after an earthquake and had been killed trying to save someone.

Poor, poor Georgie...

If only everyone knew the truth about Charlie. But how she could shatter everyone's illusions? His family and friends didn't deserve that. The way she saw it, they should be able to mourn the man they'd loved without seeing the side he'd kept hidden. Which meant she had to keep his secrets. So far, she'd managed it, because in a weird sort of way keeping that secret was protecting her, too; but she was getting to the point where she felt as if she'd explode if she didn't get away from all the memories and the pity.

So today she'd look at the website again to see if there was a match. If there wasn't a suitable match for her, she would take it as a sign to stay exactly where she was and stop being so pathetic and just get on with things. If there was a match, then it was a sign she should leave.

Location.

That meant hers: west London.

Position.

So far, so good: paediatric registrar.

Desired location.

That was harder. 'Anywhere' meant just that. And, even though she wanted to get out of London, she didn't want to go somewhere really remote. Not, she supposed, that there were that many remote hospitals. That field was probably meant for the GPs—ones who maybe wanted to swap an isolated rural practice to gain experience in the fast pace of a city practice; or maybe those who were burned out by inner-city medicine and craved a country idyll for a while.

Somewhere by the sea...

No. She could've run away to her parents' at any time, but she hadn't taken that option then and she wouldn't take it now. This was the chance to make a fresh start. She shook herself and chose the 'anywhere' option.

Time frame.

That was an easy one. Now.

Then she clicked the 'Find Your Match' button.

The system thought about it. And thought some more.

Clearly there wasn't a match, or perhaps the system was down. Georgie was about to give up and close the page when the screen changed.

One match found.

She clicked on her result. Edinburgh? She'd never been to Edinburgh.

All she really knew about the place was that it was the capital of Scotland and it had a castle, a very famous comedy festival and an amazing Hogmanay party.

One match. Meaning that this was fate giving her a little nudge to keep trying.

She clicked 'connect' and wrote a short email, doing her best to sell her job in London. And everything she wrote was true: the Royal Hampstead Free Hospital was a great place to work, her colleagues in the paediatric department were utterly lovely, and her comfortable flat in Canary Wharf with its balcony and fold-back doors overlooking the Thames was only a short walk from the Tube station.

Put like that, it would make anyone wonder

why she wanted to leave. What wasn't she telling? What was the catch in what looked like a perfect life?

The whole truth wasn't something she wanted to tell anyone, let alone a complete stranger. 'Personal reasons' was too vague and likely to net her a rejection. So, instead, she stuck to a simplified version of the truth.

I was widowed almost a year ago and I feel I need a fresh start, away from the pity.

Pity that would be so much worse if people knew the truth. Charlie had been cheating on her with Trisha for months; his mistress, who had been killed in the landslide with him, had been pregnant at the time.

In Georgie's view, nobody, but nobody, needed to know about Trisha and the baby.

She stared at the words for a while. And then she took a deep breath and pressed 'send'.

It didn't mean she was definitely going to leave. The other paediatric registrar might not want to live in this part of London, or might change his or her mind about doing the job swap. But she'd made the first move. If this didn't work out, her next attempt would be easier. And then, for the first time since she'd learned the truth about her husband, Georgie could stop feeling as if she was weighed down by the whole world.

CHAPTER ONE

Two weeks later

GEORGIE COULD STILL hardly believe it had all
happened so quickly. Clara Connolly had been
happy to swap her job in the paediatric department of St Christopher's Hospital in Edinburgh
for Georgie's job at the Royal Hampstead Free
in London, and she too wanted to start the swap
as soon as possible.

Perfect.

Telling Joshua had been the hardest part. Her
brother had been so upset. He'd accused her
of bailing on them when he and Hannah really needed her. In the end, Georgie had been
forced to tell him why she needed to get out
of London, and the truth about how Charlie
had cheated on her and lied both to her and
to his mistress. Joshua had been horrified that
she'd kept it to herself for so long, then guilty
because he felt he hadn't supported her well

enough for her to tell him the truth earlier. But they'd pretty much worked it through, he'd promised to keep it to himself, and she was going north with his blessing.

Though her brother's insistence that she should send him a text every time she stopped for a break was driving her crackers. Why did he have to fuss so much? OK, so she hadn't driven that much for a while—in London, she didn't really need a car—but she was perfectly capable of driving the seven or so hours from London to Edinburgh on her own. Actually, she was enjoying it hugely. She'd hired a bright orange convertible Mini for a fortnight, to give her enough time to work out whether to buy a car for the rest of the job swap or extend her lease; driving on the motorway on the bright autumn day, with the roof down and the stereo turned up loud with a playlist of happy, bouncy music, was the most fun she'd had in months. And she stopped every two hours at a service station to stretch her legs, grab a coffee and text Joshua that she was absolutely fine.

The navigation system was working well; not that she really needed it on the motorway, because it was pretty obvious she was just heading north up the M1 to Scotland. Apparently Clara's cottage was at the edge of a village outside Edinburgh, about thirty minutes away from the hospital; although Georgie was pretty sure she'd be able to pick up supplies in the village, she decided to get some bread, milk and instant coffee on her last stop, just to tide her over in the first minutes when she arrived.

Edinburgh.

Her new life.

Freedom.

She'd still be doing a job she loved and trying to make a difference to the world, but she would no longer have to pretend all the time. And, just in case Charlie's ghost was listening, she instructed the car's sound system to play The Proclaimers' 'I'm On My Way' and sang along with it at the top of her voice. She was definitely driving away from the misery she'd felt in London, and nothing was going to stop her enjoying her new life in Edinburgh. Being *happy.*

An hour later, she revised that.

The persistent rain had made her put the hard top on the car. It was already dark—a good hour before it got dark in London—but there were no street lights in sight so she had to rely on her headlights, and the narrowness of the road and the multiple bends meant she was driving at practically a crawl. The satnav didn't seem to have a clue where she was and kept telling her, 'You have reached your destination,' when she clearly hadn't. And she'd reversed down what felt like the same narrow, muddy track *twice* now.

Clara had said that her cottage was on the edge of the village. Obviously Clara's definition of 'edge' wasn't the same as Georgie's. Possibly neither was 'village': a pub, a church, a school, and a renovated courtyard of barns, which was apparently a farm shop and in whose car park she was now sitting as she tried to make sense of her bearings. How on earth was that a village?

Everything seemed to be firmly closed at seven o'clock on a Saturday evening—even the pub, which she could hardly believe—so she couldn't ask anyone for directions. In London, her local shops were open before dawn and closed after midnight. Did that mean she'd have to drive for half an hour to get supplies if she ran out of milk?

According to the sign on the barns, they sold fruit, veg, award-winning dairy and meat. There was a bakery and a café, and local crafts and gifts.

All crammed into a few barns in the middle of nowhere.

This was starting to feel like a huge mistake rather than a fresh start. Saturdays shouldn't be this difficult. And thank God she'd bought milk and coffee at the service station. The first thing she'd do when she got to her new house would be to put the kettle on and make double-strength coffee. Maybe treble.

OK. She'd make one last attempt to find the cottage; if that failed, she'd give in and call Clara and ask her just where the cottage was.

She drove up the narrow track as slowly as she could. And, this time, was it her imagination or was there a chink of light at the side of the road—something which might mean people? She drove even more slowly until she saw an opening that led into a yard, then carefully pulled in. There was a large four-wheel drive car already parked there, so obviously this wasn't Clara's cottage. But at least it looked as though there was someone in residence— someone who might know where Hayloft Cottage actually was and could give her directions.

She parked next to the other car, made her way to the door of the cottage and banged on it.

No answer.

But there was a deep woof. Definitely not Clara's cottage, then, because Clara hadn't said anything about a dog. A neighbour's, then. She hoped the neighbour was friendly. In London, you hardly even saw your neighbours. Would it be different here?

She knocked again. More woofing. And this

time the door was dragged open by a man who looked very fed-up indeed and was wearing nothing but a bath towel slung round his hips.

Her mouth went dry.

He had pale skin, grey eyes, slight stubble and wild, slightly over-long dark hair. Add in the light dusting of hair on his chest and his perfect six-pack, and he could've been the star of an action movie. He was the first man who'd made her mouth go dry like that since Charlie, and it put all her senses on full alert: this was dangerous.

'What do you want?' he snapped.

Oh, help. He had that lovely Scots accent too. The sort that melted your bones.

And her brain cells must have been temporarily scrambled from the long drive to make her focus on his unexpected gorgeousness instead of solving her problem. What on earth was wrong with her? The man must think she was some kind of tongue-tied idiot.

'I—I'm sorry to bother you,' she managed to get out finally, cross with herself for being so pathetic. 'I'm a bit lost. My satnav has been telling me for the last five miles that I've already reached my destination, I've been on the road since nine o'clock this morning, and to be honest I've had enough. Could you please tell me where I can find Hayloft Cottage?'

'Hayloft Cottage,' he repeated. There was another woof behind him, and he turned to the dog. 'Shh, Truffle, it's all right,' he said.

Was he scowling because he hadn't heard of the cottage? Or maybe this place was like the village where her parents lived in Norfolk, where something had an official name but everyone local called it something completely different. 'Clara Connolly lives there,' she added, hoping it would help.

'And you are…?'

'Georgina Jones—Georgie.'

'You,' he said, 'aren't due to arrive until to-morrow.'

She couldn't quite process this. What did he mean? 'Tomorrow?' she asked, confused.

'Your job swap thing. Clara said you weren't coming until tomorrow.'

'You know Clara?'

'Aye.'

The penny suddenly dropped. He knew Clara. He knew she was expected. So this had to be Hayloft Cottage. 'Are you Clara's friend? The one she said might be staying?'

For pity's sake—he knew who she was, now. Couldn't he just let her in so she could get a cup of coffee and warm up a bit?

She realised she'd spoken aloud when he raked a hand through his hair. 'Yes. Of course.

Sorry. I was in the shower. I'll get something sorted out.' His towel nearly slipped as he reached behind him to grab the dog's collar, and Georgie's pulse went up a notch. 'This is Truffle. She's a bit nervous, but she's friendly when she gets to know you.'

'Uh-huh,' she said warily.

'You're not a dog person?'

'I'd never hurt one,' she said. 'But, no, I'm not used to pets. And Clara didn't tell me to expect a dog.'

'I see.' He paused. 'Truffle's a rescue dog, so she's a wee bit shy with people she doesn't know. Ignore her and she'll come to say hello when she's feeling brave enough. She won't hurt you,' he advised. 'Though don't leave shoes or cake lying around. They'll be gone in three seconds. And please don't leave chocolate anywhere, even if you think it's out of her reach, because it won't be and it's poisonous to dogs.'

'Noted,' she said, slightly nettled by his tone. OK, so she wasn't used to dogs, but it didn't mean she was stupid. Plus it was raining and she was a little tired of being left on the doorstep by a man whose social skills seemed more than a bit on the skimpy side. So she couldn't help the sarcastic edge to her voice when she asked, 'So would it be possible to bring my stuff in, do you think?'

'Let me dry off and put some clothes on,' he said, 'and I'll help you bring your things in.'

She was perfectly capable of bringing her own things into the cottage. She wasn't a delicate little flower who needed a man to sort things out for her.

Before she could make the point, he said, 'The cottage is open-plan, so I'm afraid I can't shut Truffle in another room. Two of us bringing your things in means it'll be quicker and I won't have to keep her on her lead for so long.'

'Right.'

'Free feel free to make yourself some coffee,' he said. 'The mugs and the coffee are in the cupboard above the kettle.'

'Thank you.'

He stepped aside to let her in, then closed the front door behind him. 'Good girl, Truffle,' he said to the chocolate Labrador, then disappeared up the spiral wrought-iron staircase in the centre of the room.

So she was stuck in a cottage in the middle of nowhere with a complete stranger—one who didn't seem to be that pleased to be sharing his living space—and a nervous dog. What else hadn't Clara told her?

To be fair, Clara had said that her friend

might still be there; but she'd also said that her friend would most probably be gone before Georgie arrived. And she hadn't even mentioned the dog.

Plus Georgie had no idea what her new housemate's name was. He hadn't even introduced himself. Grumpy McGrumpface, perhaps? He might be gorgeous, but he seemed incredibly prickly. She really hoped there was a soft side to him, because sharing a place with someone difficult was going to be really wearing.

'I'm going to make some coffee,' she said to the dog, who was regarding her warily from the other side of the room.

At least with Grumpy McGrumpface leaving the room she had a chance to look round. Hayloft Cottage was compact and open plan, and utterly gorgeous. The windows all seemed quite deep-set, so Georgie guessed that the stone walls were very thick. The floors were pale flagstone, and at one end of the ground floor there was a kitchen consisting of cupboards painted sky blue, an old-fashioned butler's sink, a cream-coloured Aga and a plate rack on the wall. She assumed that the fridge, freezer and washing machine were hidden somewhere behind the cupboards. Opposite the cupboards was a scrubbed pine table and four matching chairs.

The wrought-iron staircase was the feature in the middle of the room, and there seemed to be a baby's safety gate fastened across it. On the far wall there was an old-fashioned wood burner and two comfortable sofas on either side of it with a thick rug and a coffee table set between them, plus a wicker basket with a soft blanket that clearly belonged to the dog. It was cosy and pretty, and Georgie tried not to think about the fact that it was in the middle of nowhere or how disconcerting it was not to hear any noise from passing traffic.

She headed to the kitchen area and filled the kettle. Just as Truffle's owner had said, the coffee was in a tin above the kettle, along with a shelf of mugs.

Should she make some coffee for him, too?

She was still dithering when he came downstairs. He was dry now—or at least *drier*, because his hair was still damp. And it wasn't dark, as she'd first thought: it was a deep auburn. Utterly gorgeous: but she knew that being handsome and being nice didn't necessarily go together. Charlie had been charming, but he had turned out to be far from the nice man she'd thought she'd married; and her new housemate wasn't even charming, let alone nice.

Cross with herself and knowing that she was possibly being unfair to him—for all she knew, he could've had the day from hell and the last thing he needed was a complete stranger turning up on the doorstep when he wasn't expecting her—she asked, 'Can I make you a coffee?' Once she'd downed a mug of the stuff, her head might be back in the right place again and she'd be her usual practical self. And hopefully she'd also stop reacting to him like a hormonal and star-struck teenager. She wasn't here to get swept off her feet by a handsome stranger; she was here to get her life back on some sort of track.

'Thanks. No milk or sugar.'

Did he mean he didn't take milk or sugar, or that there wasn't any? She'd organised a food delivery with a note telling Clara to use whatever she needed and to make herself at home. She'd left a bottle of decent Prosecco in the fridge and a box of her favourite truffles, with a sticky note saying 'Welcome to London'. As this was Scotland, she'd kind of hoped that Clara might have left her some shortbread as a 'welcome to the job swap' sort of thing. That hope was starting to feel a bit forlorn. And this place suddenly felt every one of the four hundred and so miles away from London, away from nearly everyone she knew.

'If you take it, sugar is in the cupboard next to the coffee and there's milk in the fridge,' he said, as if her thoughts were written all over her face.

'Thanks.' She made two mugs of coffee, then added milk and enough cold water to her own mug that she could drink it straight down, as she often did at work.

He raised an eyebrow. 'That's how my colleagues tend to drink their coffee.'

His colleagues? 'Are you a medic, too?' she asked.

He nodded.

'Clara didn't really say anything to me about you. I'm afraid I don't even know your name.' She'd been at the cottage for long enough for him to introduce himself. The fact he hadn't bothered told her that he really wasn't going to welcome her staying here.

'I'm afraid I don't even know your name.'

It was a rebuke, and Ryan knew it was deserved; though at the same time it rankled that his new housemate was judging him. He'd been thrown enough by the interruption to his shower not to think about introducing himself to her. He'd already had a really horrible shift; losing a patient always sat badly with him, and losing a patient in today's circumstances was as bad as it could get. Being polite to some posh city girl was at the bottom of the list of things he wanted to do.

'Ryan McGregor,' he said.

'Pleased to meet you, Ryan,' she said, not sounding pleased in the slightest—that made two of them, he thought—and held out her hand to shake his.

Though she was at least trying to be polite. It wasn't her fault that he'd had such a horrendous day. He ought to make the effort, too. He shook her hand, and immediately wished he hadn't when heat zinged through him.

He couldn't remember the last time he'd reacted to anyone like that, even Zoe. And he definitely couldn't afford to react like that to Georgina Jones. Especially as they were going to be sharing a house for the foreseeable future, until he could find an alternative.

The problem was, she was just his type. Petite and curvy, with green eyes and fair hair pulled back in a scrunchie, and the sweetest, sweetest smile. Gorgeous.

Dangerous.

The surge of attraction felt as if it had knocked him sideways, and he struggled to deal with it. What the hell was wrong with him? Was he going down with the flu or something? That must be why he was hot all over; clearly he had a temperature. 'Pleased to meet you, too,' he mumbled, feeling totally off balance.

'So do you work at St Christopher's?' she asked.

'Yes.'

She looked at him, her eyebrows slightly raised.

What was this, twenty questions? He stifled his annoyance. Again, it wasn't her fault that Clara had been a bit sketchy on detail. 'With Clara, on the children's ward,' he said. 'I'm acting consultant.'

Though he really wasn't in the mood for making polite conversation with a stranger. Especially one who was giving his dog wary looks. Was it the potential mud and hair she objected to? Because, in that case, she really wasn't going to enjoy a Scottish winter. Waking up to deep snow might look pretty and romantic in photographs, but the reality meant cold, wet, long journeys. Being fastidious didn't cut it, out here in the country. Designer clothing like the stuff she was wearing right now was no match for the wind and driving rain. You needed waterproofs and layers and strong boots. Had she even brought warm outdoor clothes with her? he wondered.

'I—um—wondered if you might be able to recommend a takeaway service,' she said.

'A takeaway?' Here? She had to be kidding. Did she really have no idea where she was?

'I don't mind whether it's pizza, Indian, Chinese or fish and chips. Anything,' she added, clearly trying to be helpful. Not quite snooty, then, but a bit posh and clueless. Sharing a house with her was going to be a trial, and he couldn't even let himself think about what it would be like at work. He was used to Clara, and he couldn't imagine anyone in her place.

Why was Georgina Jones even here? Did she think it would be romantic to swap her big-city lifestyle for a six-month sojourn in the romantic, pretty countryside? Maybe it'd be kindest to be a bit cruel now and burst that particular bubble. 'We're in the Pentland Hills, a good fifteen minutes' drive from the nearest big town. Even if you could talk someone into delivering it, the food would probably be cold before it got here,' he said.

'Oh.'

He knew he really ought to be nice and offer to cook something for her. But, after the day he'd had, he felt too miserable to eat. All he'd wanted to do tonight was curl up in front of the fire with his dog and maybe a small glass of single malt, and listen to the kind of bluesy rock that always soothed his soul.

Not that that was going to happen now. If

he stayed down here with his new housemate, he'd have to make small talk. And Ryan wasn't particularly interested in small talk. Especially with someone he barely knew and who didn't seem to have anything in common with him.

'I'll bring your things in,' he said, a little more abruptly than he'd intended.

'I'm perfectly capable of bringing my own stuff in,' she said, lifting her chin.

'I'm sure you are, but Truffle is a bit of an absconder and I'd rather not risk giving her the chance to disappear into the hills or find the nearest bit of fox poo to roll in,' he said. He went over to the cupboard where he kept the dog's things, took out her leash, and then coaxed the dog over to him. 'It's OK, girl,' he crooned, kneeling down by the wrought-iron staircase, and scratched behind her ears with one hand while he slipped the end of the leash through its handle, securing it to the stairs. Then he clipped the leash onto her collar. 'It's just until we get everything indoors,' he said.

The dog's ears drooped.

'I'll take you out for a walk after, I promise,' he said. He hated seeing the disappointment in the dog's eyes, the way she suddenly looked cowed and scared. Yet again, he hoped someone would find her previous owners and make sure they never, ever, *ever* owned another dog again. Just as he hoped that the parents of the four-month-old baby he'd failed to save that afternoon would never have another child, or that if they did then social services would swoop in and give them the support they so desperately needed before it was too late.

With an effort, he pulled himself together. 'Let's get your stuff in.'

Georgina's car was completely unsuitable, all style and no substance. It would cope with the track for now, but when not when the surface had turned to liquid mud. To handle the narrow track to the cottage over the winter, she'd need a four-wheel-drive, not some pretty little convertible.

And just how many suitcases did you need to stay somewhere for six months? Had she brought the entire contents of London's shoe shops with her?

Not that it was any of his business.

It was still raining, and they were both wet by the time they finished bringing in her luggage.

And Ryan was feeling really guilty. She'd asked about a takeaway service. Just because he was too miserable to eat, it didn't mean everyone else was. Clearly she was hungry.

While Georgina was unpacking, he released Truffle from her temporary confinement, then rummaged in the freezer. Clara was going to kill him. She'd left him a list of the things she wanted him to get in to give a proper Scottish welcome to her job swap partner, but he hadn't had time to do it. He'd planned to do it in the morning, before the woman arrived. It hadn't even occurred to him that she might arrive early. There was half a loaf of bread in the freezer, some peas, a bag of chips, and an orange lump in a plastic box that might be homemade soup, except it didn't have a label and it was probably way past its use-by date.

The fridge was just as empty. It held milk and half a lump of cheese, and that was about it.

Grimly, he promised himself he'd go shopping for food tomorrow.

Georgina Jones had been on the road since nine this morning—and this wasn't the proper Scottish welcome his best friend had planned. He'd let Clara down.

Just as Clara had let him down.

He shoved the thought away. Clara had done what was right for her, and he wasn't going to stand in his best friend's way. OK, so she felt like the only stable thing in his life right now apart from Truffle, but that wasn't her problem. And after all these years he should be used to being on his own. Used to the fact that people in his life tended to leave him—and that was his fault, too, because he couldn't let people close. He couldn't trust them not to leave him; his mother had died when he was six, her family hadn't wanted him and a string of foster parents had given up on him. He'd thought at one point that Zoe might be the one to change things; but he'd ended up pushing her away, too, and she'd left him—which pretty much proved he'd been right in the first place. Relationships weren't for him.

Though now wasn't the time for a pity party. He was absolutely fine on his own. He had his job, he had his dog—who was pretty much his whole family—and he had friends. He shook himself mentally. What did he call this woman, anyway? Georgina? Georgie? Dr Jones? *Hey, you*, was definitely wrong.

And why the hell was he worrying so much about this? Nothing fazed Dr Ryan McGregor. Well, almost nothing. Social niceties hadn't bothered him for years. Why should a woman he hadn't met until a few minutes ago put him in such a spin? How utterly, utterly ridiculous.

'Dr Jones?' he called. 'I can make some cheese on toast.'

She appeared halfway down the stairs. 'Seriously?'

He understood why she sounded so snooty. Cheese on toast wasn't exactly a proper meal.

But then, if she'd wanted a proper meal she should've turned up on the day she'd agreed, not the day before. 'I was expecting you tomorrow,' he said. 'I haven't had time to go shopping. Cheese on toast—or just toast, if you don't eat cheese—is all I can offer.' He resisted the temptation to add, 'And you're lucky I'm offering that.'

For a moment, she looked shocked, even dismayed. But then she recovered and gave him a very professional-looking smile. 'That'd be good. Thank you.'

This really, really wasn't what he'd promised Clara he'd do, and guilt prickled through him. 'I might have some soup to go with it.' He crossed his fingers, hoping the orange gloop from the freezer really *was* home-made carrot soup. He couldn't think what else it would be.

'Can I do anything to help?'

He wasn't sure whether she was being polite, or assuming that he was as useless at preparing meals as he was at organising them. In either case, he didn't want her under his feet. He didn't really want her here at all, if he was honest; he just wanted to be on his own so he could decompress. 'No. You've just driven up here from London. A day early,' he couldn't help pointing out.

'It's the day I agreed with Clara.'

No, it wasn't. He suppressed a sigh. 'You're meant to be here on Sunday the sixth.'

'Saturday the fifth,' she corrected.

'Clara wrote it on the kitchen calendar. The one where we write our shifts so we know when each other's working.' He walked over to the pinboard next to the cabinets, the dog trotting at his heels. 'See? Sunday the— Oh, crap.'

'What's wrong?' she asked.

'I assumed the calendar was like the one on my phone and started on a Monday, not a Sunday. So at a glance it told me you were arriving on Sunday, not Saturday.' He groaned and raked a hand through his hair. What the hell was wrong with him? He paid scrupulous attention at work. Nothing got past him. So why, when it came to his home life, was everything such a mess? 'I apologise.'

'It's OK.' Though the look she gave him could've curdled milk.

The next six months were going to feel very, very long indeed.

Thankfully she left him alone to make the food, though he also noticed that she didn't go and make a fuss of Truffle. Not a dog person, then. Her loss.

He thought of his nightmare case earlier and wished he could've turned the clock back. To the point where someone had noticed what had been going on in that house and given them enough support to stop it happening, or removed the baby into temporary care before it was too late. OK, so his own experience of foster care had been less than great—but foster care was still better than living in a house where someone might hurt a child.

The orange gloop in the box wasn't soup. It turned out to be mango sorbet. 'Oh, crap,' he said when he tasted it.

'What's wrong?' she asked.

'I don't think mango sorbet is meant to be heated.'

'No.' The word was expressionless—as was her face—but he'd seen the slight contempt in her eyes before she'd masked it.

Christ. Why hadn't he just asked Janie at the farm shop to drop off some supplies for him today? Probably, he thought wryly, because he'd been in a bit of denial that Clara was actually going and he was going to have to get used to someone else as a housemate until he found a place of his own.

He'd keep his promise to Clara later and organise a welcome meal for her job swap partner. Though he hadn't agreed to anything about actually *sharing* said dinner with the new housemate, so he could get Janie to sort out a touristy dinner for him, stick it in the microwave to heat it through for Dr Snootypants, and then take Truffle out so he didn't have to see the woman sneering at the local delica—

The smell of singed bread brought him back from his thoughts and he yanked the pan from under the grill.

Crap, crap and double crap.

Not only was the orange gloop not soup, he'd managed to burn the cheese on toast because he hadn't been paying attention.

Annoyed with himself, he cut off as much of the singed bits as he could, and dumped the edible bits on a plate.

'Cheese on toast,' he said, handing her the plate.

'Aren't you having any?' she asked.

'I'm not hungry.' He thought again of the baby who hadn't made it, the mum who'd dropped to her knees as if felled by an axe and wailed her loss into the floor, the dad who'd been white-faced with guilt and shame and horror and mumbled incoherent apologies.

No. He really, really wasn't hungry.

'I'll leave you to it,' he said, knowing he was being rude but just not being able to face making conversation.

'Thanks.' She took a breath. 'Is it OK to have a bath after I've eaten?'

'You mean, have I hogged all the hot water?' he asked, nettled.

'No. I mean I've had a long drive, I'm tired, and I could do with a bath and an early night.'

'Oh.' He'd been oversensitive and assumed she'd meant something she actually hadn't. 'Sorry,' he muttered. 'Sure. There are towels in the airing cupboard next to the bathroom, and the water's hot.'

'Thank you,' she said.

'I'll leave you to it,' he said again. 'I'll take Truffle out.'

She didn't make any anodyne comment about seeing him later. Which was absolutely fine by him. He didn't particularly want to make conversation with her. He pulled on a waterproof coat and wellies, then clipped the dog's leash to her collar and left. And hopefully when they got back she'd be in bed and he could just sit down with his dog and a glass of single malt, as he'd originally planned on his way home from the hospital, and get his head back into a better place.

Without the man who was the walking cliché of a dour Scotsman and his equally unfriendly dog, the cottage should've felt larger. Instead, it felt smaller. How weird was that?

Georgie hadn't really expected a housemate;

and to have one who was so abrasive *and* had a nervous dog was… She blew out a breath. It was something that she wasn't going to tell her brother about, because otherwise Joshua would worry. Maybe she ought to make more of an effort with Clara's friend; but then again, Grumpy McGrumpface hadn't exactly made a lot of effort to be friendly with her, had he?

He'd made her something to eat, yes, but he'd done it with bad grace and even worse ability. The so-called cheese on toast was utterly inedible. She wasn't even going to try to choke it down. Or the heated-up sorbet, which in other circumstances she would've found hilarious but right now she just found irritating. Ryan McGregor might be pretty to look at, but she had the feeling he was going to be the housemate from hell.

She scraped the revolting mess into the bin with a grimace. Just as well she'd bought bread at the service station. She made herself a couple of slices of toast—which she ate dry, because there wasn't any butter in the fridge, let alone anything else to spread on toast—then headed upstairs for a bath. Tomorrow was another day. And maybe tomorrow she'd see the really pretty side of Scotland, the reason she'd moved up here from London.

Though, when Georgie peered out of the window after her bath, she saw complete darkness. Scarily so. She couldn't even see the shapes of the trees in the neighbouring field against the night sky. And it was so *quiet*. There wasn't so much as an owl hooting; then again, would an owl bother flying around in all this rain? It trickled down the windowpane relentlessly.

Scotland was so very different from London.

Didn't they say you should be careful what you wished for? Georgie had wished to be out of London, and here she was. So she should just stop whining and try to see the good side of things, the way she normally did, instead of staring into the darkness and wondering if she'd just made a huge, huge mistake. But it really did feel like a mistake, now she was sharing a cottage in the middle of nowhere with someone who didn't really want her here and found it an effort to be polite, instead of living in her luxury flat with its stunning views over the river, with her elder brother and her niece only a couple of floors away in the same building. Why hadn't she appreciated it more? Was work going to end up being difficult, too?

Though she couldn't just give in and go home. She'd have to make the best of it.

The next morning, she showered and changed into a sweater and jeans, then peered out of the window to see blue skies scattered with fluffy white clouds—and actual hills. The view from Hayloft Cottage was amazing, hills and heather stretching out as far as the eye could see; but it also made her wonder how Clara was getting on in London. Had Clara, too, had a rough first night—kept awake by the noise of the traffic and the river and the brightness of the street lamps, in the same way that Georgie had been kept awake by their complete opposite?

Ryan was nowhere to be seen when she went downstairs. Neither was his dog. OK. If she left now, she wouldn't have to put up with his dourness when he came back. She'd drive into the city, check out where the hospital was so she was prepared for her first shift tomorrow, and then grab something to eat, do a bit of sightseeing, and find a supermarket.

She scribbled a note to say she was going out and would be back later. Then she locked the door behind her, climbed into her car, and headed for the city.

She loved her first view of Edinburgh, when she drove down the Royal Mile in the Old Town, with the castle looming over it and the Palace of Holyroodhouse at the bottom, and then through to the New Town with its sweeping Georgian terraces that reminded her a lot of Bath. St Christopher's Hospital was utterly gorgeous, a Georgian building made from mellow golden stone, with huge sash windows and a big triangular pediment above the front door and columns flattened against the wall either side.

Hopefully her colleagues would turn out to be as lovely as the building.

Once she'd worked out where the staff car park was and was sure she knew where she was going first thing tomorrow, she headed back into the centre of town and parked.

The first thing she was going to do was tick off a couple of things on her tourist wish list.

Edinburgh Castle was a good place to start; according to the internet search she'd done back in London, it would give her amazing views of the city, plus a chance to see the Honours of Scotland—the Scottish Crown Jewels—and the firing of the gun on the roof at lunchtime. She thoroughly enjoyed wandering around the castle. Costumed interpreters and the 'court musician' made it even better, and she loved the huge medieval hall, the jewels, the ancient Stone of Destiny and the spectacle of the gun firing.

She took a few photos to send to her brother, her parents and her best friend with the caption:

How amazing is this? Right decision to come to Bonnie Scotland!

A sandwich and a cup of tea revived her, and then she headed to the supermarket.

Did she shop for one or two? She had no idea what kind of arrangement Clara had with Ryan, and she had no idea what Ryan ate. Was he vegetarian? Did he have any allergies?

Maybe she'd cook for him today, as a way of trying to reach some kind of understanding with him. She didn't need him to be her new best friend; but being on civil terms would make both their lives a lot easier.

She had no idea what his shift pattern was; he'd said something about writing it on the calendar, but she hadn't thought to check the calendar before she'd left for the city. OK. She'd cook something that she could reheat quickly, if necessary. A chicken and vegetable stew, so she wouldn't have to bother cooking the vegetables separately, and she'd serve it with microwaveable rice. A jar of pasta sauce and some dried pasta, too, in case he didn't eat chicken, and anyway it was always useful having some store-cupboard essentials for a quick meal. She paid for her shopping and then drove back to the cottage.

There was no sign of Ryan's car; when she opened the front door, there was no sign of the dog. She put the shopping away, and then she noticed the note on the table.

At the hospital.
Truffle with Janie.
Back later.
R

Who was Janie? His girlfriend?

Not that it was any of her business.

She glanced at her watch. It was a mile down to the village. Hopefully she could have a quick look round and take some snaps to send home, and be back here before it was dark.

She was about to lock the front door when her phone pinged.

The text was from Clara.

Thanks for the bubbles, chocolate and food order! London's great. Sorry for not warning you earlier about Truffle. She's a sweetheart but keep your shoes locked up because SHE CHEWS.

Pretty much what Ryan had said.

Georgie texted back.

I'll remember.

Hope your welcome dinner was nice. Ry's not the best cook.

Georgie blinked. Welcome dinner? But then, it wasn't Clara's fault that Ryan was difficult. She didn't want to make her job swap partner feel bad. Though now she was seeing the funny side of the heated-up mango sorbet and burned cheese on toast, it would be nice to have someone to laugh about it with. She was pretty sure that Ryan wouldn't see the funny side.

It was lovely, she lied. It's very pretty out here.

And you're getting on OK with Ryan?

Oh, she really couldn't tell the truth about that one.

Just fine.

Time for some deflection.

Good luck with your first shift tomorrow.

You, too.

So Clara had asked Ryan to make her a welcome dinner? Even though he hadn't, Georgie thought that maybe she ought to ask Joshua to do something nice for Clara. It wasn't her job swap partner's fault that her housemate had let her down.

She walked down to the village and took a few snaps, then followed up with a text to Joshua, complete with pictures to show him how gorgeous the village was, and asked him to sort out something nice for Clara; and then sent the same pictures to her parents and to Sadie, her best friend.

The farm shop was still open, so she decided to go and have a quick look around. It was an amazing place, full of fresh food, local artwork and jewellery, and even some locally made cosmetics; she picked up an adorable knitted dachshund for her niece Hannah, and some enamelled earrings and honey hand cream that she knew her mum would love.

But when she went to pay, she saw the dog curled up in a basket next to the till. 'Truffle?'

The dog gave a thump of her tail. Just one, but at least it was recognition of sorts.

The woman at the till looked at her. 'Now, lass, I don't know you, but you clearly know our Truffle, so would I be right in guessing that you're my new neighbour—the London doctor who's swapped jobs with our Clara for six months?'

'Yes,' Georgie said. 'Georgina Jones—though please call me Georgie.'

'Nice to meet you, Georgie,' the woman said. 'I'm Janie Morris. You might see our sheep peering through your window at some point.'

Georgie blinked. 'Sheep?'

'My Donald and I run the rare breeds farm as well as the shop,' Janie said, 'and our sheep are in the field next to Hayloft Cottage. They're a wee bit nosy. Welcome to Scotland.' She rang Georgie's purchases through the till. 'My mum knits the dogs.'

'It's for my niece,' Georgie said.

'I hope she'll love it.' Janie took a thistle-shaped piece of shortbread and wrapped it deftly in greaseproof paper. 'Here. Something to have with your coffee. I made it myself this morning.'

'Thank you.' Georgie was shocked to find herself close to tears. This was the nearest thing she'd had to a welcome since coming here, and it made her feel ridiculously homesick.

'Now, I know Clara and Ryan work all hours, so I'm guessing you'll be the same. If you need milk or bread, or you want me to put anything by from the deli for you, just send me a text and I'll drop it off. I'm only next door and I've got a spare key, just as you and Ryan have mine, so it's no trouble. We can sort out the money side of it later.'

'That's so kind of you,' Georgie said. 'Thank you.'

'Ryan will give you my number,' Janie said.

And that was where this whole thing would fall down. Georgie couldn't imagine Ryan doing anything to help. He was way too prickly.

'He's a nice boy, Ryan,' Janie added.

Maybe in a parallel universe Ryan was nice, but Georgie smiled in lieu of contradicting her new neighbour. Least said, soonest mended.

'I assume you came to collect Truffle?' Janie asked.

How did she explain that she'd had no idea Truffle was here—Ryan had said the dog was with Janie, but not who Janie was—and she knew nothing about dogs? 'I, um—yes.' Then she thought of a nice way of saying no. 'That is, if Ryan left her lead?'

'He did.'

No excuses, then. She'd have to collect the dog, now.

Janie smiled at her. 'And you've some poo bags?'

'No,' Georgie said.

'That's no bother. I have some here.' Janie took a couple of bags from a drawer.

'Thank you.'

'I often look after Truffle for Ry, when he's at work,' Janie said. 'She's a good girl. Shy, but a sweetheart.'

When she produced Truffle's lead, Georgie was left with no choice but to take the dog back to the cottage with her. And Truffle did the biggest poo in the world, halfway up the lane. Followed by another one about twenty steps later. Oh, great. This wasn't Bonnie Scotland, it was more like Pooey Scotland, she thought wryly. She left the two bags on top of the dustbin when she got back to the cottage—hopefully Ryan would tell her where to dispose of them when he got back—and looked at the dog.

'I have no idea what to do with you. I don't know if I'm supposed to wipe your feet, or anything. So just please, please, don't do anything that will upset Grumpy McGrumpface, and I will do—oh, whatever it is that dogs like. Not that you can tell me. But I'll find out.'

The dog regarded her solemnly.

'All righty. Let's go in.'

Once inside the cottage, Truffle went straight to her bed. Though, when Georgie started making the chicken stew, the dog ventured into the kitchen area and lay down on the floor, looking hopefully at Georgie.

'I'm not sure if I'm allowed to give you anything,' Georgie said. 'How about I put a bit of chicken to one side for you? Then I'll ask your owner if you can have it.'

Truffle wagged her tail, just once. Obviously the dog didn't have a clue what she was saying, Georgie thought—but it was nice to kid herself. To feel that at least someone here wasn't totally averse to her presence.

Christ, what a day. Reliving everything from the previous day, taking the police through everything he knew and everything the team had done to try to save the baby.

Ryan still couldn't forgive himself for failing.

When he parked in the courtyard and walked into the farm shop, he was surprised not to be greeted by his dog.

'Young Georgie collected Truffle earlier,' Janie informed him. 'She's a lovely lass.'

Dr Snootypants, more like. But maybe she'd been nicer with Janie than she had with him.

'She bought one of Mum's knitted dogs for her niece,' Janie added. 'I think she'll be good with the children on the ward.'

She'd better be. Otherwise he was going to ask for a replacement. 'Right. Well, thanks for looking after Truffle for me. I appreciate it.'

'I know you do, and you helped Donald fix the fence last weekend. That's what neighbours are for,' Janie said.

When Ryan walked into the cottage, Truffle bounded over to him, wagging her tail. And the house smelled amazing. Whatever Dr Snooty-pants was cooking, it was fabulous. Way, way above his own skill set.

'Hi,' she said, looking up from the sofa, where she seemed to be reading a magazine.

'Hi.' She'd picked up his dog so he needed to be pleasant to her, even though he wasn't feeling it. 'Thank you for picking up Truffle. I wasn't expecting you to do that.'

'I just walked her back here. She's been asleep a lot of the time.'

'Uh-huh.'

'I left the poo bags on top of the bin, because I didn't know where to dispose of them.'

She'd picked up poo? Now, that he hadn't expected. 'I'll sort it,' he said.

'Um, and I cooked dinner,' she said. 'It'll take five minutes to heat through.'

'Thanks, but you don't have to cook for me.'

'I don't know what arrangements you had with Clara,' she said, 'but it would make sense for us to share the chores.'

He grimaced. 'I'm not a great cook.'

'Clara said.'

He felt his eyes widen. 'You've talked to Clara?'

'She texted me and said she hoped my welcome meal was good.'

He hadn't even looked at his phone. No doubt there would be a text from his best friend asking what the hell he thought he was doing. 'Sorry,' he muttered, guilt flooding through him. He'd let Clara down—and he hadn't welcomed her job swap partner at all.

'I said,' Georgie added, 'that it was lovely.'

Something else she hadn't had to do: lie, to save his bacon. 'It was terrible.'

'It was different.' Her lips twitched at the corners. 'It's the first time I've been offered hot mango soup.'

For a second, he wasn't sure whether she was laughing at him; and then he realised that she was laughing at the situation.

And she had a point. It *was* absolutely ridiculous.

Shockingly, he found himself smiling back. 'I'm sorry,' he said. 'Maybe we got off on the wrong foot. I'm Ryan McGregor. Hello.'

'Georgina Jones, but everyone calls me Georgie.' She got up from the sofa, and an unexpected wave of lust surged through him. Her skinny jeans showed off her figure to perfection. Georgie Jones was *gorgeous*.

And, when she shook his hand, again he felt that weird connection. It scared him as much as it surprised him; he hadn't expected to react to her in that way. He didn't want to, either; what was left of his heart definitely needed protecting.

'Good day?' she asked.

The aftermath of yesterday. It'd been far from good. 'It was OK,' he lied. And, before she could ask for more detail, he needed to distract her. 'You got on all right with Truffle, then?'

'Yes. I wasn't sure if you allowed her to have treats, so I didn't give her any of the chicken when I made the stew. But I did cook some and put it aside for her, in case you said yes.'

Again, she'd gone above and beyond, side-swiping his expectations. 'That was kind of you. She'll love it. Thanks.'

She shrugged it aside. 'I don't know what to do with dogs. But I already know no chocolate, and keep her away from shoes.'

'Like I said, I've had to replace three pairs, so far.'

'I'll remember to keep my shoes out of her reach. We're going to be all right with each other—aren't we, Truffle?' Georgie asked.

God, her mouth was pretty when she smiled. Soft and warm and inviting. It made him want to reach out and draw his thumb along her lower lip.

He shoved the thought away. This really wasn't the time or the place. And it was completely inappropriate.

'So she's a rescue dog?' Georgie asked.

'Abandoned,' he said. And it still broke his heart when he thought about it. He hadn't meant to say any more, but suddenly it came spilling out. 'No collar, no microchip. She was about six months when she was dumped. We think her original owners couldn't cope with the demands of a puppy, so they brought her to the middle of nowhere and left her. She tried to find her way home; she was nearly hit by a car when she found the main road, but thankfully the driver stopped in time, coaxed her into his car and took her to the nearest dog shelter.'

'Poor thing,' Georgina said.

'Indeed,' he said drily.

'How long have you had her?'

'Just over a year.'

'So she's about eighteen months old now?'

'Nearly two years,' he said. And again he found himself explaining. Something about Georgie's serious green eyes made him want to talk; which was weird, because he never reacted to strangers like that. He rarely opened up to his friends, either. What the hell was going on?

'She was rehomed, but she's a chewer—I'm

guessing her first owners didn't occupy her enough, and when she's bored or stressed she tends to chew things. The people who took her on really wanted to keep her, but they had small children who didn't enjoy having their teddy bears stolen and shredded, so they brought her back to the shelter after the first couple of weeks and she ended up with me.'

'It was good of you to take her on.'

Truffle had been just as good for him. It had been Clara's suggestion and his best friend had been right, because having the dog around had really helped him through his divorce. His dog was the only real family he had now. Not that he planned to tell Georgina about his divorce or his past. 'She's a good dog. But because of her past she has a few trust issues.' Which was why he understood her so well.

'The house I planned to buy fell through at the last minute, and most rental places don't allow pets—especially a dog who's known to chew. And I don't want to put Truffle in kennels where she'll think I've abandoned her.' Because he knew just how it felt to be abandoned: again, not that he was going to tell Georgina about that. 'She needs to know her for ever home is with me. That's why Clara offered to let me stay with her for a bit, though the stair gate's there to stop Truffle going upstairs,' he said instead.

'That's kind.'

'That's Clara. She's lovely.'

She tipped her head to one side. 'You're close to her?'

Closer than he'd been to most people. Which was why it hurt so much that she'd done the job swap thing without even talking to him about it beforehand. She hadn't trusted him with how she was feeling; and he hadn't been a good enough friend to notice something was wrong. 'She's my best friend. The sister I never had.' Like the family he'd never had—and they hadn't stayed with him, either.

Georgie thought about it. The sister he'd never had. Right now, she guessed that Ryan was feeling as frustrated and angry with Clara as her own brother was with her. But maybe this job-and-life swap thing meant that Clara would support Joshua if Georgie would support Ryan.

'I'm a stranger,' she said, 'and I know next to nothing about dogs. But Clara and I are pretty much swapping lives. She'll be getting used to my life in London, and I'll get used to her life here. We're going to have to make the best of sharing. If you're really the world's worst cook, then I don't mind doing the cooking for both of us—but then the washing up will be your department.' She'd spent years being the one who did everything, to keep life easy; from now on, it was equals or nothing.

'That,' he said, 'sounds fair. Clara and I have a rota. We can tweak it to suit.'

'That's fine with me.' She paused. 'I stocked the fridge a bit. I wasn't entirely sure what to get, because I didn't know if you're vegetarian or have any allergies. If chicken stew isn't OK, I can cook pasta with tomato sauce tonight.'

'Chicken stew,' he said, 'is absolutely fine. No allergies and I'm not fussy.' Foster care had taught him very quickly not to be fussy about food. 'Thank you. And either I'll give you half of what you spent in the shop, or you give me a list and I'll pay for the next shop, so it's fair shares.'

'OK. I'll heat the stew and the rice and serve dinner at six,' she said. 'I'll, um, see you in a bit.' And she disappeared upstairs to her room.

Ryan was quiet and a bit distant when they ate.

The last time she'd shared a house with someone she didn't know was more than a decade ago, when she'd been a student. Making conversation had been so much easier back then: you'd ask your fellow students about their home town, their A-level subjects and their course, and then you'd talk about music and TV and films and establish what you had in common. She couldn't really do any of that with Ryan; it felt too much like being nosy. Still, she had a good excuse for an early night. 'I'm on an early shift tomorrow, so I'll head for bed.'

'I'm on a late,' Ryan said. 'I would offer to take you into the hospital tomorrow morning, but there isn't a bus back here, so you wouldn't be able to get home until my shift finishes.'

'I'll be fine driving myself in,' she said. 'I did a recce earlier today. See you tomorrow.'

'See you tomorrow.'

He wasn't quite as abrasive tonight as he'd been the previous day, but there was definitely something upsetting him, Georgie thought. Something that had made those grey eyes full of misery. And he barely knew her, so he was hardly going to confide in her.

She wasn't going to brood about it. Or start asking about him: because she didn't want her own past becoming common knowledge and gossiped about, either.

At least she was starting at the hospital tomorrow. Once she was actually doing her job, something she was familiar with, she'd feel a lot better.

CHAPTER TWO

THE JOURNEY INTO work was lovely, with the sky streaked with pre-dawn colour. Georgie managed to park without a problem, then was introduced to everyone by the head of the Paediatric Department, had a copy of her rota from the department's secretary, and got straight to work in the Paediatric Assessment Unit.

'I'm Parminder—everyone calls me Parm,' the nurse in the assessment unit told her with a smile. 'I'm rostered on with you in the PAU today. Welcome to St Christopher's.'

'Thank you.' So not everyone at the hospital was going to be as difficult as Ryan, then. That was a relief. 'I'm Georgina, but everyone calls me Georgie.'

'So are you settling in all right, Georgie?'

'I think so. It's very different from London— I wasn't expecting to be living somewhere quite so rural,' Georgie admitted.

Parminder smiled. 'At least you're sharing a house with Ryan. He's such a sweetie.'

Were they talking about the same person? Ryan most definitely wasn't a sweetie, in Georgie's experience. He'd opened up to her a bit about his dog the previous evening, but he didn't seem to have much of a sense of humour, and she felt as if she was treading on eggshells around him. 'Uh-huh,' she said, trying her best to sound noncommittal.

'He's really good with the staff. All the students love him,' Parminder said.

Why? Just because he was really good looking?

As if she'd asked the first question out loud, Parminder told her, 'He's always got time to explain things to them, and he's really good with the kids. And he treats the nurses with respect instead of behaving as if we're much lesser mortals.'

Ha. He'd behaved as if *she* was a lesser mortal.

'Mind you, he's been so quiet, this last year. Ever since his divorce. And he doesn't seem to have found anyone to share his life since then.' Parminder wrinkled her nose. 'Sorry. I shouldn't be gossiping.'

'Don't worry. I won't repeat anything you

said,' Georgie reassured her. Though she didn't quite feel up to explaining that she and Ryan weren't exactly saying much to each other.

'And he's had a horrible weekend—I don't mean with you arriving,' Parminder said hastily, 'but that poor baby on Saturday morning.'

'Baby?'

'Didn't he tell you?' Parminder winced. 'We had a little one in with a non-accidental head injury.'

'Oh, no.' Georgie went cold. That was the sort of nightmare case every paediatrician dreaded.

And it made things drop into place: everyone she'd spoken to seemed to think that Ryan was lovely. But nobody would be lovely after a case like that. It was the sort of thing that would make anyone short-tempered. Perhaps that was why she and Ryan had got off to such a rocky start.

'He had to come in yesterday to talk to the police,' Parminder said. 'And I guess it's the sort of thing you think about over and over, wondering if you could've done something differently to change the outcome—even though I don't think anyone could've done any more than he did.'

This didn't sound good. She had to ask. 'The baby didn't make it?'

Parminder swallowed hard and shook her head.

'I'm sorry,' Georgie said, feeling guilty about the way she'd reacted towards Ryan on Saturday. *Grumpy McGrumpface.* She'd had no idea. She would never have been so frosty with him if she'd known he'd had such an awful day. No wonder he'd seemed all over the place on Saturday night, incapable of even making cheese on toast. She'd just assumed he wasn't happy about sharing the house with her and was being difficult on purpose.

Then again, he hadn't told her what had happened, so how could she possibly have known? She wasn't a mind-reader.

'It's not your fault, hen.'

It still didn't sit well with her. But right now there was nothing she could do to solve it, and she had a job to do. 'Let's see our first patient,' Georgie said with a smile.

That morning's caseload was similar to those she'd dealt with at the assessment unit in Hampstead: rashes, head injuries, a Colles' fracture and the first of the winter's bronchiolitis cases. But Georgie found herself really struggling to understand her patients' parents. In times of stress, anxious parents often gabbled their words, but with a strong Edinburgh accent on top Georgie found herself needing to ask people to repeat themselves over and over again.

Her new colleagues were kind and asked her to go to lunch with them in the staff canteen, but again she found them hard to understand; was it her, or did *everyone* in Scotland speak really quickly? Nearly all the conversations seemed to revolve around football and rugby—things she knew nothing about—or about people she didn't know, and she found herself growing quieter and quieter as the break went on.

How was she going to cope with six months of this? And how could she learn to fit into such a different environment? Back in London, everyone talked about movies and music and gin. She knew what she was doing there. Here…she felt really out of the loop.

It seemed she was going to have to learn a bit about football, she thought. And maybe she could try a charm offensive tomorrow. Bring in some brownies—which maybe she should've done today.

She called in to pick up some ingredients from the farm shop on her way back to the cottage, and discovered that Truffle was there.

'Are you sure you don't mind taking her

home, lass?' Janie asked. 'Ry mentioned this morning that you weren't used to dogs.'

'I'm fine,' she said with a smile. And she could always vacuum the dog hairs out of the car.

'I haven't had a chance to walk her, mind. If you could?' Janie asked.

It couldn't be any harder than the previous day. At least now she had a better idea of what to expect. 'Can I buy some poo bags as well?' Georgie asked. 'It's just I'm not sure where Ryan keeps them.'

'Don't worry yourself, lass. Here.' Janie handed her a roll of poo bags. 'They're on the house. And I'm guessing it would matter to you, so I can reassure you they're the biodegradable sort and not the ones that just clog up the landfill.'

'Thank you. That's good to know.'

Truffle didn't seem to mind jumping in the back of the car, and Georgie dropped the bits she'd bought back at the cottage before taking the dog out for a walk.

'It's as much to clear my head as to exercise you,' she told the dog. 'It was one hell of a first day, even though the patients were all easy. I like my colleagues, but half the time I can't understand what they're saying. They must all think I'm stupid.' She sighed. 'And Ryan. I had no idea he'd had that terrible case on Saturday. Maybe it'll be easier between us this evening.'

They were back at the cottage before it got dark, and Georgie made a fuss of the dog before baking a batch of brownies and making a veggie chilli. 'It's hard to make friends when you can't even follow what everyone's saying,' she said to the dog. 'And, apart from Parminder, I got the impression that none of them think I'm up to Clara's standards. Or maybe I'm just being paranoid. I guess we'll just have to get used to each other.'

The dog nudged her, as if to say, 'Like you and me.' Georgie smiled and scratched the top of Truffle's head. 'Yeah. You're right. Tomorrow is another day.'

She microwaved half a pack of basmati rice to go with her portion of the chilli, and fed Truffle a cup full of the kibble she'd found in the cupboard. The dog curled up on the sofa next to her while she flicked through the TV channels.

'I have no idea if you're allowed up here,' she said, 'but if you don't tell Ryan, neither will I.' Having the dog leaning against her, sharing warmth, felt surprisingly good. If anyone had told her five years ago that she'd quite enjoy having a dog around, she would've laughed.

But she was rapidly becoming very fond of Truffle. There was a lot to be said for quiet companionship.

Ryan came in a couple of hours later.

'Good evening,' she said.

'Good evening. Thank you for picking up Truffle. Janie texted me,' he said.

'It's fine.' She paused. 'I made a veggie chilli—there's a bowl in the fridge and half a packet of microwaveable rice.'

'Thanks. That was good of you.'

'It's what we agreed.' And, if she was honest with herself, she'd missed cooking for two. 'And there's a brownie on the plate.'

'From Janie?'

'No. I made some for the ward tomorrow. But I kept the chocolate well away from Truffle.' She paused. 'Parm told me about your case on Saturday.'

His face shuttered. 'Yeah.'

'That's hard.'

'Yeah.'

She folded her arms. For pity's sake, would he give her a break? 'I'm *trying* to be nice.'

He shrugged. 'I'm a guy.'

She'd noticed, though she stuffed the awareness right back in the box where it came from.

She wasn't ready to notice his masculinity. She didn't need any complications in her life.

'And guys don't talk about things? That's so stupid.' She shook her head. 'Talking's a good safety valve. It helps us cope when we have a case that breaks our hearts.'

He looked at her. 'Or it makes us relive it.'

'As you wish. But some food might make you feel better. I've fed Truffle, by the way. I looked on the pack and weighed out what they said was the middle of the range for a dog her size. I hope that was all right.'

'Thank you.' He looked surprised. 'That was kind.'

'I could hardly feed her veggie chilli,' she pointed out drily.

'No, because onions and garlic are toxic for dogs.'

'Did you used to take your bad days at work out on Clara?' she asked.

'I…' He closed his eyes for a moment. 'No. Sorry. That isn't fair of me.'

At least he admitted it. She pushed down the fact that Charlie had never admitted when he was in the wrong. Charlie was dead and buried, along with a lot of her hopes and dreams. 'Sit down,' she said. 'I'll microwave stuff, and you talk. Otherwise it's going to fester in your head and you won't sleep tonight.'

'You're bossy,' he said.

She inclined her head in acknowledgement. 'Sometimes you have to be.' She busied herself sorting out the chilli and rice while he sat down, then put the bowl in front of him.

'Thank you,' he said. And then he didn't speak for a while, except to mutter that the chilli was good.

When his bowl was empty, she folded her arms. 'No brownie until you talk. And, just so you know, I make seriously good brownies. You'd be missing out on a lot.'

'Uh-huh.'

'Unless you're holding out for a dipping sauce of hot mango sorbet to go with it?'

For a moment, she thought she might have gone too far, but then he laughed.

And oh, that was a mistake.

When he wasn't being grumpy, Ryan McGregor was the most gorgeous man she'd ever met—including Charlie, in the years when she'd been young and starry-eyed and hopelessly in love. Ryan's grey eyes stopped being stony when they were lit with amusement, his face changed entirely when he wasn't being all brooding and severe, and his mouth suddenly looked warm and soft and tempting.

And she'd better stop thinking that way, because she wasn't in the market for a relationship. This six months in Scotland was all about getting her head straight and finding herself again, getting back to a place where people would just stop pitying her.

'I'll pass on the hot mango. But yes, please, to a brownie.' He paused. 'Saturday was grim. I take it Parm told you that the baby didn't make it?'

She nodded.

'It's the worst thing ever, when a baby dies,' he said. 'And it makes you feel so angry and so helpless, all at the same time. The parents were young and they didn't get the right support.' He closed his eyes briefly. 'Part of me wants to see them locked up for ever—I hate losing patients, and circumstances like these make it worse—but it's not my job to judge them. When you've got a baby who won't stop crying so you haven't slept properly for weeks, and you don't know what to do to stop the baby crying, and you're frustrated and miserable and desperate, sometimes you react in a way you wouldn't do if you were in your right mind. If you don't ask for help, or you don't know how to…' He blew out a breath.

'Well. There's a young man right now who has to live with the consequences of what he did for the rest of his life. A family ripped to pieces. A funeral to plan. Everybody loses.'

'What happened?' she asked softly.

'The parents brought him in, saying he'd had a fit. They didn't know what to do. I was trying to find out if anything like that had happened before, or if there were any warning signs they hadn't known to look for, if there was a family history—and then the mum broke down. It seems the baby woke them a lot during the night and the dad went in when the baby started crying in the morning... And he shook the baby.'

Georgie felt sick. A momentary snap with life-changing consequences. How would they ever forgive themselves—or each other?

'The eye exam showed retinal bleeding, but the blood tests didn't show up any bleeding or genetic disorders,' Ryan continued softly.

She knew what he was going to say next. 'And the scans showed subdural haemorrhage and encephalopathy?' Together with the retinal bleeding, it was the triad that usually proved non-accidental injury.

'The surgeon tried a shunt to reduce pressure in the baby's brain, but...' He shook his head. 'We need to do more to support vulnerable parents. Teach them that it's fine to ask for help. That the crying won't go on for ever, even though it feels like it—and, when it gets too much, then you just put the baby safely down in the cot and walk away for ten minutes, give yourself a chance to cool down. Call someone. Do breathing exercises. Sing. Throw a cushion. *Anything* that helps you cope and keeps the baby safe.'

'Agreed,' she said softly. She reached across the table and squeezed his hand briefly. 'I'm so sorry.'

'Me, too. And I'm sorry I wasn't very nice to you when you turned up.'

'You'd had the shift from hell, and you weren't expecting me. And I wasn't very nice to you, either.'

'Dr Snootypants.'

She felt her eyes widen. 'Is that what you called me? Well, *you* were Grumpy McGrumpface.'

'Grumpy McGrumpface?' He stared at her in seeming disbelief, and for a moment she thought they were about to get into another slanging match.

But then he nodded. 'You have a point. I was miserable after my shift, guilty because I'd got it all wrong about when you were supposed to arrive, and the whole thing just snowballed. The snootier you were with me, the angrier I got.'

'And the more you acted as if I was a nuisance, the more sarcastic I got with you. We both got it wrong,' she said. 'Maybe we should cut each other a bit of slack and start again.'

'I'm still not a great cook,' he warned. 'When it was my turn to sort dinner, I served up ready meals. I bought them from Janie, mind, so it was as good as home-cooked, but I do micro-wave dinners only.'

'We'll work something out between us,' she said, and finally handed him the plate with the brownie. 'Eat this. From what Parm said, no-body could have done any more than you did on Saturday.'

'That doesn't make it feel any better. I still couldn't save the baby.'

'We all get cases that haunt us,' she said softly. 'Things we can't fix, no matter how hard we try, because they're just not fixable.'

'Is that why you're here?' he asked. 'Because you needed to get away from memories in London?'

Yes, but not quite how he thought it was.

It seemed that Clara had respected her confidence, and Georgie was grateful for that. But what did she do now? On the one hand, she didn't want him to think that the move here was just an idle whim. On the other hand, if she told him even part of the truth, there was a risk she'd end up having to field all the pity here as much as she had in London. What was the point of coming four hundred miles to repeat your mistakes?

He was looking at her curiously, his amazing eyes full of questions.

'It's personal,' she hedged.

'Uh-huh.' But he didn't try to fill the gap with small talk. He waited.

In the end, she caved. 'All right. But, if I tell you the truth,' she said, 'I want you to promise me on your honour as a doctor that it stays confidential. And,' she added, 'most importantly, I want you to promise you're not going to start pitying me.'

He looked surprised, then nodded. 'All right. You have my word.'

Was that enough?

She thought about it. She barely knew him, and the fact she hadn't picked up on the fact that her husband was a liar and a cheat showed that her own instincts weren't so great. But she'd heard the way Ryan's colleagues and his neighbour spoke about him. They seemed to think he was a man who could be trusted; and that decided her in his favour. She'd take the chance.

'I love my job and I love my family and I love my friends. But, last year, my husband was one of the emergency doctors on a rescue mission after an earthquake, and he was killed in an unexpected landslide.' She couldn't bring herself to tell Ryan the rest of it. About the baby her husband had made with his mistress, though he'd come up with excuse after excuse not to make a baby with her. Better to stick to a simplified version of the truth. 'Everyone at work was sympathetic and kind, but I hate being seen as "Poor Georgie"—it's been weighing me down. I know everyone means well, but the pity just stifles me. And I needed to get a break from it all. That's why I wanted to leave London.'

Ryan could understand that. It was exactly how he'd felt after his marriage had crashed and burned. Everyone had been so nice, and he'd been so miserable. Clara had been his rock, offering him and Truffle somewhere to stay until he could buy another house—Zoe had bought him out of their home—but, oh, the conversations that had stopped when he'd walked into the room and the pitying glances. He'd hated being talked about, even though he'd known people were trying to be kind rather than judging him.

'I get that,' he said softly. 'And I won't pry. It's none of my business.'

'Thank you.'

Telling him about her husband's death had

clearly been painful. But in some ways she'd done them both a favour: she'd given him another reason to keep a bit of emotional distance between them and not give in to the growing attraction he felt towards her. Physically, she was gorgeous, but it was more than just looks. Something about Georgina Jones made him feel hot all over, made him feel like a teenage boy having his first crush.

And that wasn't a good thing.

He wasn't good at relationships. He already had one divorce under his belt—and he knew that the break-up of his marriage was largely his own fault. He hadn't let Zoe close enough, and he hadn't been able to put his own feelings aside to give her the family of her dreams. As a widow, Georgie was clearly grieving for her late husband and she didn't need the complication of getting involved with a man whose own heart was a complete and utter mess.

'Given that I'm not Clara, will sharing a house with me be a problem?' she asked.

'Problem?' Did she mean because she wasn't Clara, or that he had a girlfriend who might not be happy about his new housemate? Unless someone at the hospital had filled her in, she wouldn't know. He took a deep breath. OK. She'd been honest with him. He'd be honest with her. Plus perhaps he needed to reassure her that he wasn't going to see her as easy prey. 'I'm divorced, and I'm not looking for another partner. So you'll be quite safe with me. You'll be staying in Clara's room and we both have our own bathrooms.'

'Thank you—though I'm not looking for another partner, either,' she said. 'You're safe with me, too.'

So why was it that he didn't feel safe in the slightest? What was it about Georgina Jones and her clear green eyes that made him feel he needed to build an extra barrier around his heart, and build it fast?

He shook himself. 'Well. Now that's out of the way, perhaps we can be good—' No, friends wasn't the right term. 'Housemates,' he finished.

She lifted her mug of coffee. 'I'll drink to that.'

Something reckless in him made him say, 'I have a better idea if we're drinking to something.' He went over to the cupboard and extracted a bottle and two glasses.

'I'm afraid I'm not really a whisky drinker,' she said when he brought them over to the table with a small jug of water.

'This isn't like the stuff you get in the supermarkets,' he said. 'It's a properly matured single malt. Try a sip—and then try it with a little water. It'll be smoother and let the subtle flavours come through.'

'Trust you, you're a doctor?' she asked wryly.

'Something like that.' He poured a small amount of the amber liquid into the two glasses, handed one to her and clinked his glass against hers. 'To housemates.'

'To housemates,' she echoed, and took a tiny sip.

When she grimaced, he added a little water to her glass. 'Try it now.'

'Oh—that's very different,' she said, looking surprised. 'It's quite nice. I can't believe that a little bit of water makes that much difference.'

'I won't bore you with the full details, but one of my housemates at university was a chemist,' Ryan told her. 'He wrote his dissertation on the smokiness of whisky and what affects the flavour, and he tested out his theories on the rest of the house.'

'Sounds like fun,' she said. 'So did you study in Edinburgh?'

'Yes, and I trained here, too. I assume you went to London?'

'Yes. I followed in my brother's footsteps,' she said. 'Actually, I work with him now. Technically, he's my boss.'

'And he was OK about your job swap?'

'We had a bit of a fight about it,' she admitted. 'He thought I was making a mistake.'

'And you don't?'

'No. I needed a change,' she said. 'Though I do feel bad about deserting him.'

'Clara's an excellent doctor and she gets on well with everyone. She'll do a great job,' Ryan said.

'I don't mean professionally,' she said. 'I'm Joshua's back-up for Hannah—his daughter,' she clarified. 'He's a single dad. He does have a nanny, but I'm there if he needs me. He lives in the same apartment block as I do, a couple of floors up.' She bit her lip. 'I feel guilty for being here because I've deserted them. But if I'd stayed in London I would've gone crazy.'

Yeah. He'd been there. Truffle had got him through the worst bits. The loneliness and the misery and wondering why he couldn't be the man his wife needed. But he'd come to terms with it now. He was who he was. And if that meant being alone, so be it. 'Sometimes you need to do what's right for you, even if it puts someone else out.' Which was, at the end of the day, all Clara had done, too. 'Your brother will forgive you. Since he worked with you, he must've seen how all the pity was getting you down.'

'Maybe.' She yawned, and blushed. 'Sorry.

It's either the whisky or all this country air. And I'm on an early tomorrow. I'm off to bed.'

Ryan had to stifle a sudden picture of her curled up under the duvet, her hair spread over a pillow. *His pillow.*

For pity's sake. He was too old to start suffering from insta-lust. And he was just going to ignore the physical attraction. Nothing was going to happen between them. She was a widow. Still grieving. She'd made it very clear that she wasn't looking for a relationship. He didn't want one, either: he had no intention of setting himself up to fail all over again.

So he'd just have to look a bit harder to find a house that would suit him and Truffle, and put a little bit of distance between himself and Georgie as soon as he could.

CHAPTER THREE

'YOUR NEW HOUSEMATE'S a bit on the quiet side,' Alistair, one of the junior doctors, said to Ryan on Tuesday morning when they grabbed a cup of coffee in the staff kitchen.

'Georgina's all right,' Ryan said.

'But she's not Clara, is she? She's not the life and soul of the party.'

'It's early days. Give her a bit of time to get used to us. Anyway, the most important thing is how she is with the children,' Ryan reminded him.

'Aye, and their parents,' Alistair agreed.

It made Ryan think, though, when he was back in his office, wrestling with paperwork. Being the new person in the department wasn't much fun. He hadn't made anywhere near enough effort at making her welcome; he hadn't even done the welcome dinner he'd promised Clara he'd sort out. Georgina had been really kind to him yesterday, when he'd opened up about his nightmare case. It was his turn to show some kindness and include her in the department a bit more. Maybe he could organise a team night out or something.

Georgina Jones had clearly had a rough year, being a widow. So he needed to do what Clara would do, and make his new colleague feel at home. He pushed aside the thought that it wasn't the only reason why he wanted to make her feel better. Yes, she was physically attractive. And the way she'd teased him about hot mango sorbet had made him feel lighter of spirit, a feeling he'd forgotten; part of him wanted more, but part of him was scared spitless at the idea. He'd failed in his marriage, and it wasn't as if Zoe was difficult. She wasn't high-maintenance or spoiled; she'd just wanted him to love her and make a family with her, to raise children with her. They weren't whims or wishes out of the ordinary.

Yet he hadn't been able to do it.

He'd loved his wife, but he just couldn't let down his barriers enough to let her properly close, the way a husband should. He didn't want children and he knew he'd be rubbish as a father—with his past, how could he be otherwise? He hadn't a clue how a real father behaved.

Having a family with his wife should've been

the easiest thing in the world. He hadn't done it. His relationship had crashed and burned. And how much harder would it be to start a relationship with someone who'd experienced such a terrible loss already? Where he might not measure up against her late husband?

So it was better not to let his thoughts even go there. Whatever his libido might like to hope, it wasn't going to happen.

Georgie had a case that worried her. Baby Jasmine was a day and a half old, and had been feeding well so she'd gone home with her mum the day before; but, unlike most newborns, she'd slept completely through the first night. This morning she was lethargic, not opening her eyes. When the midwife arrived for her follow-up visit, Jasmine still wouldn't feed and then she started trembling. On the midwife's advice, Jasmine's parents had brought her straight into the paediatric assessment unit at St Christopher's.

Small babies could get very sick, very quickly; and Georgie really wasn't happy when she noticed Jasmine's breathing becoming more rapid.

It could be dehydration, it could be a blood sugar level problem, or it could be a virus. But, most importantly, she needed to keep Jasmine's breathing supported. She called up to the special care baby unit to get Jasmine ventilated and monitored, and ordered a battery of tests.

But later that morning all the tests came back clear. No dehydration, no blood sugar problems, and none of the other obvious things.

What was she missing? Some kind of allergy, perhaps?

She really needed input from someone with more experience. Even though the person she needed help from wasn't the easiest to deal with, her patient's needs came first. So she went to find Ryan in his office. 'Dr McGregor, do you have a moment, please?'

He looked up from his desk. 'What can I do for you?'

'I've got parents in with a very sick baby and I can't work out what's wrong. As you have more experience than I do, I was hoping you might see what I'm missing,' she said.

He nodded. 'Run me through it.'

She explained Jasmine's symptoms. 'I've got her on prophylactic antibiotics, in case it's a bacterial infection, but the SCBU says she's unresponsive, her face is swollen, she's deteriorating, and there just doesn't seem to be a reason for it because all the tests have come back clear.'

'A swollen face,' he said thoughtfully. 'Given

that she's a newborn and there's progressive lethargy, it might be a urea cycle disorder. It's pretty rare—maybe one in a hundred thousand babies suffer from it, so that'd be six or seven each year in the UK—but try checking her for argininosuccinic aciduria.'

'So get her blood tested for ammonia?' she asked. At his nod, she added, 'I'm on it. Thanks.'

'Let me know how it goes,' he said. 'And it's nearly lunchtime, so would you like to grab a sandwich with me?'

That was the very last thing she'd expected. He'd done his best to avoid her at the cottage. Had he had some kind of sea-change and decided to make her feel welcome in Edinburgh? Or was this the real Ryan, the man she hadn't met yet—the man Parminder had said all the team adored?

She decided to give him the chance. 'If you could tell me everything you know about argininosuccinic aciduria, then yes, please,' she said. 'Otherwise, I'll be spending my lunchtime online, researching it.'

'Come and get me when you've ordered the tests,' he said. 'You've enough time for a sandwich and coffee before the results come back, and I'll fill you in.'

She sorted out the tests, then went to the canteen with him.

'How are you settling in, other than having a case that would make anyone panic slightly?' he asked.

'OK. I'm starting to understand more of the accent up here, provided I can persuade people to slow down a bit when they talk.' She gave him a rueful smile. 'And I think I'm going to have to learn a lot about football.'

He grinned, surprising her—and she was also shocked to feel as if her heart had just done an anatomically impossible somersault. When he was nice, he was very nice indeed. Then again, she knew his flip side: Grumpy McGrumpface.

Behave, she told her libido silently. *He's off limits*.

'Be very careful about which team you pick,' he said.

'London?' she asked hopefully.

He laughed. 'Which gives you at least fifteen to choose from.'

'I think,' she said, 'I'll have to find a list of them and toss a coin.' And she needed to concentrate on work, before her libido got the chance to have control of her tongue and came out with something inappropriate. 'So can you run me through argininosuccinic aciduria?'

'It's an autosomal recessive trait where the child lacks the enzyme argininosuccinic lyase,' he said, 'so that means either both her parents are carriers, or one of them maybe has the late onset form.'

'So between them they would have a one in two chance of a child being a carrier, a one in four chance of the baby having the condition, and a one in four chance of the baby not being affected at all,' she said.

He nodded. 'Symptoms usually start at birth, but might not be noticed for a few days. If it's less severe, it might start later in childhood or even adulthood. The lack of the enzyme causes excess nitrogen in the blood, in the form of ammonia.'

'Which damages the central nervous system. So that's why she'd be lethargic, refusing to eat, and her breathing's too fast,' Georgie said thoughtfully.

'I'd check her liver, too,' he said. 'And there's also a risk of neurological damage.' He paused. 'If it *is* argininosuccinic aciduria, would you like me to talk to the parents with you?'

'As I've never come across a case before, yes, please,' she said.

'I've only seen one case,' he said, 'when I was a student. But the baby was fine and he still comes in to see us regularly, so that should help reassure Jasmine's parents.'

'Is there a support group?' she asked.

'Yes, so we can give her parents the details.'

'Thank you.' She finished her coffee. 'Sorry to be rude, but I'd better get back. I won't be happy until I get those test results.'

The results provided the answer: there were indeed raised levels of ammonia in Jasmine's blood. Georgie went to the SCBU to update them and start treatment for Jasmine, then went to find Ryan. 'Thank you. Your diagnosis was spot on,' she said.

'Let's go and see her parents,' he said.

She introduced him to Jasmine's parents. 'Dr McGregor's the acting consultant in the department, and thankfully he's seen a case like Jasmine's before, so he was able to suggest different tests and we know what's wrong now,' she said.

'So is she going to d—be all right?' Jasmine's dad corrected himself, looking anxious.

It was the big fear of every parent with a newborn, and her heart went out to him.

'We're treating her now, so hopefully she'll start turning a corner today,' Ryan said reassuringly.

'So what's wrong with her?' Jasmine's mum asked.

'It's something called argininosuccinic acid-uria,' Georgie said. 'It's caused by an enzyme deficiency.'

'When your body digests protein, the protein is broken down by enzymes into amino acids, and some of the acids turn into ammonia,' Ryan explained. 'Usually ammonia is excreted from the body when you urinate, but the enzyme deficiency means that Jasmine's body can't do that so the ammonia builds up in her blood.'

'Can you treat it?' Jasmine's mum asked.

'Yes. She's still very poorly and it's going to take a couple of weeks before she'll be able to come home again,' Georgie said, 'but we know what it is now, so we can give her the right treatment.'

'First of all, we need to filter her blood to get rid of the ammonia,' Ryan said, 'and then we need to find the right balance of milk protein feeds and medication to keep her ammonia levels under control.'

'And she'll be all right?' Jasmine's dad asked.

'There can be complications, but she should be fine,' Ryan said.

'Argin—' Jasmine's mum shook her head.

'Argininosuccinic aciduria,' Georgie repeated.

'I've never heard of it,' Jasmine's mum said.

'It's rare—about one in a hundred thousand

babies get it—but there are children living perfectly normal lives with the same condition,' Ryan reassured her. 'When I was a student, I treated a baby with it here, and he's doing just fine. He's at high school now.'

'Is there a family history of any urea cycle disorders for either of you?' Georgie asked.

Jasmine's dad shook his head. 'Not that I know of—though my parents had a little boy about six years before I was born, and he died when he was a couple of days old. They thought it was cot death.' His face filled with terror. 'Oh, no. Does this mean he had the same thing that Jasmine has, this argino thing?'

'It's a possibility,' Georgie said, wanting to reassure him, 'but the difference is that we know what it is, so we're treating her and she's not going to die. If your brother had it, it sounds as if nobody picked up on it and he didn't get treatment.'

Jasmine's mum looked awkward. 'I'm adopted, so I don't know if there's anything in my blood line. I'm not in touch with my birth family.'

Georgie squeezed her hands. 'It's fine. We can offer you some tests to see if either of you is a carrier or has a problem with the enzyme, and if that's the case then if you have more children we'll know to test the baby straight after the birth.'

'I'm just so…' Jasmine's mum dragged in a breath to cut off the words.

'Of course it's scary,' Georgie said. 'She's a day and a half old. But she's in the right place and you both did all the right things. You brought her here in good time.'

'We're giving her the right treatment and we're expecting a good outcome,' Ryan said, 'but I do need to tell you that sometimes argininosuccinic aciduria can cause neurological damage. Right now it's early days so we can't give you a definitive answer, but it might be that because of what's happened Jasmine takes a little bit longer than average to reach the baby milestones—rolling over, sitting up, that sort of thing.'

'But we're keeping a very close eye on her,' Georgie said. 'Once we've got her stabilised, we can work with a dietician to find out the right amounts of protein and medication she needs. You can give her the medicine with an oral syringe, just as you would with infant paracetamol. Though you'll need to monitor every single thing she eats, and she'll need regular follow-up appointments as she grows to make sure that she's still getting the right amount of protein and medication.'

'It sounds a bit daunting,' Ryan added, 'but it's workable.'

'We'll do everything we need to, to keep her well,' Jasmine's mum said.

'Everything,' Jasmine's dad agreed.

'That's great. We can also give you an emergency plan to follow if she picks up a bug that makes her sick or gives her diarrhoea, which will obviously affect what she eats and how her body processes it,' Georgie said. 'The main thing is, you're not alone. We're here, and we can put you in touch with a support group so you can talk to other parents whose families have been through exactly what you're all going through, and they can reassure you and give you practical advice.'

'We really appreciate that,' Jasmine's mum said. 'So can we see her now?'

'Of course you can. She's got a lot of tubes and cannulas in,' Georgie said, 'but you can sit by her and talk to her and stroke her head and hold her hand. I know it's not quite the same as cuddling her, but she'll know you're there and it'll comfort her.'

'And our nurses are more than happy for parents to be involved in their babies' care, so you'll be able to help with things like washing her face and changing her nappy,' Ryan added.

'I'll take you up and introduce you properly,' Georgie promised.

'Thank you,' Jasmine's parents said, looking relieved.

'It looks scarier than it actually is,' Ryan said. 'But just remember that Jasmine will get a little bit better every day. Before you know it, she'll be back home.'

Georgie popped into the special care baby unit after her shift, too, just to see how Jasmine was getting on; and then she drove back to the cottage, pleased that her second day had gone well. Even though it was raining again, everything was fine until she was heading up the track to the cottage; then she felt a jolt, and after that the car started to pull strongly to the left-hand side.

Oh, no.

She was pretty sure that meant the car had a puncture. She'd never actually been in the car with a puncture before. Her dad had shown her how to change a tyre, but that had been years ago and she could barely remember how. The middle of a muddy track, in the rain, when it was starting to get dark and there was no place for anyone to pass her so she was completely blocking the road, wasn't exactly the best place to change a tyre for the first time.

Not that she had any other options. She'd just have to get on with it.

She stopped the car, put her hazard lights on to warn anyone else who might need to use the track that she was there, and used her phone as a torch so she could inspect the wheels on the passenger side of the car. Just as she'd feared, there was a hole in the front tyre; clearly she'd damaged it when she'd bumped through the pothole. Changing the tyre it was, then.

But, when she looked in the well of the boot, the spare wheel she'd expected to see wasn't there. All she could see was a repair kit with a compressor and a bottle of goo. According to the packaging, it would act as a temporary repair until she could get the car to a garage or tyre fitter to replace it, as long as the hole in the tyre was less than four millimetres in diameter and the side wall of the tyre was fine. Otherwise the kit wouldn't work and the tyre would have to be changed.

She went back to measure the hole. Six millimetres. She blew out a breath. Great. The repair kit wouldn't work and she didn't have a spare wheel. Now what?

The rain was coming down a lot faster now, and the wind was getting up, driving the rain right into her. She was soaked to the skin—

and she was stuck here until she could get that tyre changed.

Shivering, she climbed back into the car. Please let there be a signal for her phone, so she could call a roadside assistance service. She wasn't sure if they'd come out to people who weren't actually members, but she hoped at least they'd be able to put her in touch with someone who would come out and help.

Then she noticed the sticker on the corner of the windscreen: it seemed that the hire car came with membership of a roadside assistance service. One hurdle down.

Though her relief was short-lived. When she rang them, they advised that they couldn't come out to rescue her for three hours.

Three hours.

She was tired, she was wet, she was cold, she was starting to get hungry, and right at that moment all she really wanted was a hot shower and a cup of tea. Clearly she was going to have to wait for a lot longer than she wanted to. But other people had much worse to contend with; she was lucky, she reminded herself, and she had a lot to be thankful for.

A few minutes later, she became aware of headlights travelling up the track behind her, and then she heard the sound of a car horn.

Time to upset the neighbours, she thought

ruefully, and jumped out of the car, ready to apologise for the fact that she couldn't move her car and it was still going to be another couple of hours before the assistance company could rescue her.

Then she recognised the car.

Ryan.

'Georgie? Are you all right? What's happened to your car?' he asked, climbing out of the car to join her.

'I've got a puncture—and the hole's too big for the repair kit to work,' she said. 'Sorry, I know I'm blocking the track, but I'm afraid it'll be another couple of hours before the assistance company can get to me.'

'Do you want me to change the tyre for you?' he asked.

'Thanks for the offer, but there isn't a spare— just a repair kit,' she said.

'Ah, the joys of modern cars.' He rolled his eyes. 'Which tyre?'

'Front left.'

He went to inspect it, then came back. 'You're right—the repair kit definitely won't work on that. Look, I know the track well so I can avoid the pot holes more easily. Do you want me to drive your car back to the cottage for you?'

She bit her lip. 'Isn't that going to—well—cause problems with the car if you drive it on a flat tyre?'

'Not if I take it very slowly and carefully,' he said. 'Why don't I drive it back and you follow me in my car? Then you can wait for the assistance guys at the cottage.'

The offer sounded genuine rather than grudging, and he wasn't sneering; so it would be sensible to accept. It meant she could have a hot shower and dry clothes and a cup of tea. 'Thank you. I accept.' What she really wanted was a hug, but she was pretty sure that asking Ryan for a hug would be a step too far.

Without further comment, he handed her his car keys, then drove her hire car down the track.

Georgie followed him in his car—and discovered that Ryan listened to really loud rock music when he drove. He'd seemed so closed off that she'd expected him to drive in silence, or listen to podcasts on developments in paediatric medicine. But rock music… That was something they had in common, even though she preferred the poppier end of the spectrum. Maybe that would help them connect better and make the house-share easier.

Back at the cottage, she rang the assistance

company to tell them she'd moved the car. When she came downstairs from the shower, Ryan was standing by the kettle.

'Thank you for rescuing me,' she said.

'No bother. Go and sit by the fire and keep Truffle company. I'll bring you a cup of tea. How do you like it?'

Just for a moment, she was really, really aware of the curve of his mouth. How sensual it was. How soft his lips looked. Then she shook herself, realising that he was waiting for an answer. An answer about *tea,* not about how she liked to be kissed. Oh, for pity's sake. She needed to get a grip. Ryan McGregor was the last person she should be fantasising about. 'Medium strength, a bit of milk and no sugar, please.'

'Done. Sit yourself down.'

When Georgie sat on the sofa next to the fire, Truffle curled up by her feet, as if to try and warm her up a bit. Georgie reached down to stroke the top of the dog's head, and the dog licked her hand.

This was so far from her life in London.

And, now she was safe and warming up again, she was beginning to think that maybe there was something good about the wilds of Scotland. Something that would help to finally heal the sore spots in her heart.

* * *

Ryan busied himself making two mugs of tea.

Georgie had looked so lost, so vulnerable, when she'd got out of the car. And he'd really had to stop himself from wrapping his arms round her, holding her close and telling her that everything would be OK.

He already knew that she hated pity.

Though this wasn't pity. It was something else. Something he didn't want to explore too closely, because he knew there could be no future in it. Georgie was going back to London in six months' time; and in any case he wasn't looking for any kind of relationship. That would be the quickest way to get his heart broken again—well, not that he had much of a heart, according to Zoe, because he hadn't been sympathetic when her biological clock had started ticking unexpectedly. He'd reminded her that they were both focused on their careers; she'd countered that people could change their minds.

He couldn't change his. He just couldn't see himself as a father.

And deep down he thought there was something wrong with him. Something unlovable. OK, so his mum had only left him because she'd been knocked off her bicycle by a car and hadn't recovered from the head injury; but after she'd died her parents had rejected him, and none of his foster parents had been prepared to work with him.

The only two real constants in his life were his best friend—Clara, whom he loved dearly, but as a sister rather than as a life partner—and Truffle.

He was quite happy as he was, just him and his dog. Nobody to desert him again. He wasn't lonely, deep down. He *wasn't*.

Ryan shook himself mentally and took Georgie's mug of tea over to her.

'Thanks. You've no idea how much I fantasised about this when I was standing in the rain, staring at the hole in my tyre,' she said.

Not as much as he'd been fantasising about what her mouth might taste like.

He pushed the inappropriate thought away. 'What's the news on Jasmine?' he asked. Work at least was a safe topic.

'She's holding her own. Hopefully she'll start to turn a corner now. And thank you again for your help with the case.'

'No problem.' He paused. 'You're good with parents. Reassuring.'

'I hope so.' She grimaced. 'Though I let them down with the diagnosis.'

'This was rare—it's only the second case I've seen,' he said. 'And you came straight to me and asked for help instead of putting your patient at risk.'

'Of course I did. Our patients should always come first,' she said. 'So I'd always ask someone with more experience rather than trying to muddle through and getting it wrong.'

Ryan liked her attitude.

He liked *her*, too. And he was going to have to squash the feelings that were starting to seep through every time he looked at her.

Thankfully they were interrupted by the roadside assistance company, who'd brought a spare wheel and sorted out the car for her. By the time she came back in, he'd got his wayward feelings firmly back under control and compartmentalised everything. And now life was just how he liked it: with no complications.

CHAPTER FOUR

THE NEXT MORNING, Georgie made coffee and bacon sandwiches for breakfast, to thank Ryan for rescuing her the previous evening.

'I hope my dog hasn't been pestering you,' Ryan said, eyeing the Labrador sternly.

She had, but Georgie didn't want to drop the dog in it. 'I hope it was all right to give her a tiny bit of bacon. She looked so pleading—and I can't resist those big brown eyes.' She didn't think she'd be very good at resisting a certain pair of grey eyes, either; but that would mean trusting someone again, and finding out about Charlie's betrayal had really knocked her ability to trust, so it was better not to start something she couldn't finish.

'A little bit of bacon's fine,' he said with a smile. 'You're getting used to her, then.'

'And she's getting used to me.' Georgie was surprised to realise how much she was enjoying having a dog around. Why had she never thought of getting a pet before?

Then, when she reached to take another sandwich from the plate, her hand brushed against Ryan's—and it felt as if she'd been galvanised.

'Sorry,' she muttered, pulling away. But, when she looked up, there was a slash of colour across his cheekbones—as if he, too, had been affected by that brief touch. For a moment, her brain felt scrambled and she didn't know what to do or say. They were almost strangers. Most of the time they'd spent together so far, they hadn't even got on well. But she was very, very aware of how good-looking Ryan was—especially when he smiled.

He'd already told her he was divorced and he wasn't looking for a partner. She wasn't looking for a partner, either. So it was disconcerting to find herself wondering, *what if?*

She pulled herself together—just—and said lightly, 'I'm on a late shift today, so I'm going in to see the car hire people this morning to ask if they'll swap the car for me.'

'Good idea,' he said. 'I'll organise dinner.'

'It's OK. I'll have something at work,' she said.

'I promised Clara I'd do you a welcome dinner,' he said. 'I'm not planning to make it myself. I'm buying it from Janie's.'

Refusing would be throwing his welcome back in his face. And, as they were just starting to get on, she didn't want to risk going back to how it had been on her first night here. 'OK. Thank you. I don't have any allergies or major dislikes.'

'So that's haggis for two, then?'

The Scottish national dish: Georgie knew haggis was a kind of pudding made from sheep's heart, liver and lungs, mixed with onion, oatmeal and suet. She'd never tried it, but she wasn't sure she could bring herself to eat it.

'I, um…' She bit her lip.

He grinned. 'Don't tell anyone, but haggis isn't really my thing, either.'

He'd been teasing her? She looked at him, outraged. And then that awareness crept back in. The little nudge of her subconscious, wondering what a candlelit dinner with him would be like, The cottage would be all romantic and gorgeous in the soft light; and maybe then he'd put some music on and they'd dance together…

Oh, help. She was really going to have to get a grip. Fantasising about her housemate was a bad idea.

'I'd better go,' she said. 'I cooked breakfast, so you're on dish duty.'

And that little bit of sassiness was enough to

break the spell and stop her blurting out something stupid.

She managed to sort out the car; and her shift was calm until late afternoon, when a mum rushed in with her four-month-old baby, looking distraught.

'Lewis has got a temperature, and a rash that won't fade, and...' She dragged in a breath.

'Let's have a look,' Georgie said gently, recognising the signs of panic and wanting to calm her patient's mum down. 'Hello, gorgeous boy.'

The ear thermometer confirmed that he had a fever, and when she gently undressed him the rash was obvious—but it didn't look like the meningitis rash that his mum was clearly worrying about.

'So how long has Lewis been ill?' she asked.

'I've thought he was coming down with something for the last three or four days,' Lewis's mum said. 'He went off his food, he's got a bit of a cough and he's been grumpy. I thought it was just a cold starting, but then I saw the rash and I just panicked.'

'I can tell you now it's not the meningitis rash.' Though Georgie wasn't going to worry the poor woman further by pointing out that meningitis wasn't always accompanied by a rash. 'Did he have any spots in his mouth yesterday? Greyish-white ones?'

'I don't think so, but I'm not sure.'

'OK. Did the rash start at his head and neck?' Lewis's mum nodded.

'I think he has measles,' Georgie said. 'Do you have any other children?'

'Yes, a two-year-old and a four-year-old.'

'May I ask if they've had the vaccination?' She crossed her fingers mentally, hoping that the answer was yes; otherwise there was a strong chance the poor woman would have three under-fives at home with measles next week.

'Yes. My gran had measles when she was small and it left her deaf in one ear, so I had the boys vaccinated and made sure they had their boosters. Lewis was going to have it when he's old enough. I…' She shook her head. 'How can he have *measles*?'

'Measles has come back in the UK over the last couple of years,' Georgie said. 'It's a mixture of people not giving their children the booster vaccination, or thinking they don't need it because measles isn't around any more, and then visiting other countries where measles is rife. It's pretty contagious, so maybe you've been somewhere with other children and one of them was coming down with it and their mum didn't realise because the rash hadn't come out yet.'

'It must've been at the wear-'em-out play place we went to on Saturday. I let Jake and Ollie run about and do all the slides and the ball pit, and Lewis was asleep in his pram.' She bit her lip. 'So Lewis could end up deaf, like his great-gran?'

'Hopefully not,' Georgie said.

'Can you give him anything to stop it? Antibiotics?' Lewis's mum asked.

'I can give him immunoglobulin, which will give him a short-term boost of antibodies and then hopefully the virus will be less serious,' Georgie said. 'Measles is a virus, so antibiotics won't do a thing to help, and I'm afraid you just have to let it runs its course. The good news is that Lewis should be better in about a week, but try to keep him away from others if you can for the next three or four days, to avoid spreading the infection. How much does he weigh?'

'Seven kilos—dead in the middle for his age.'

'That's great. It means he's big enough for you to be able to give him paracetamol to help get his temperature down; and you need to give him lots of cooled boiled water to drink,' Georgie said.

'What about his cough?' Lewis's mum asked.

'He's too young for honey and lemon, and frankly cough mixture won't help him—your best bet is to put him in a steamy bathroom for a few minutes, or put a wet towel over the radiator in the room,' Georgie advised. 'If his nose is blocked, you could try giving him nasal saline drops—that'll help thin the mucus, so he'll find it easier to drink. But not all babies tolerate the drops well, so you might find it makes him worse.'

Lewis's mum looked anxious. 'And you think he'll be all right in a few days?'

'Yes,' Georgie said. 'But if you think he's developing an ear or eye infection, or he's got diarrhoea or vomiting, go to your GP—ring them first, though, to warn them he has measles, because it's really contagious. And if he's struggling to breathe or it's painful, or he coughs up blood, then bring him straight back here.'

She sorted out the immunoglobulin injection and administered paracetamol, then printed out an information leaflet for Lewis's mum to take home.

The rest of her shift was less eventful, and she drove back to Hayloft Cottage; once she was out of the city, away from the lights, she could see the stars; they were so much brighter than they were in London, and she couldn't remember the last time she'd seen the sheer beauty of the night sky like this. Even though she missed London, she was beginning to see why Clara loved it out here.

When she got back to the cottage, Truffle greeted her with a waggy tail and Ryan actually smiled at her. Her stomach swooped, just as it had this morning when they'd accidentally brushed hands.

'So how was your day?' he asked.

'Fine—apart from a four-month-old baby with measles.'

'Ouch.' He winced.

'I gave him HNIG, so hopefully that will lessen the severity,' she said. 'Fortunately his siblings had had both vaccinations, so they should be OK.'

'It's shocking, seeing measles back in the hospital,' he said. 'Apparently there were four times as many cases in the first three months of this year as there were last year.'

She nodded. 'The poor mum saw the rash and thought it might be meningitis—thankfully it wasn't, though measles is serious enough. Her grandmother's hearing was damaged by measles, so she's well aware of what it could do. Oh, and you'll be pleased to know that Jasmine's responding well to treatment. I popped up to see her before I came home.'

'That's good to hear,' he said.

'Something smells nice.' And it was strange

to come home to someone else making dinner. Charlie had always left everything to her. Ryan had said earlier that he only did ready meals, but it was good not to be the one who had to do all the thinking and the planning and the preparation.

'Can I do anything to help?' she asked.

'No, you're fine. Sit down.'

The first course was smoked salmon from the farm shop, served simply with a salad drizzled with honey and mustard dressing. 'It's locally bred and locally smoked,' he confirmed.

It was followed by Scottish beef in beer, a pale yellow mash Ryan told her was 'neeps and tatties'—a mix of swede and potato, mashed with butter and black pepper. And then the last of the local raspberries, with the most amazing salted caramel ice cream.

'It's lovely,' she said. 'And it's so nice to have someone else sort out dinner for me. Charlie never cooked or did housework.'

Which was pretty selfish, Ryan thought, since they'd both been full-time doctors. Yet Georgie didn't seem like the sort who'd let someone get away with behaving like that. She'd definitely bitten back when Ryan had pushed her too far.

'Was he an expert at burning food, too?' he asked lightly.

'No. I don't think he knew where the toaster was kept, let alone how to use it. He just...' She grimaced. 'Never mind. You shouldn't speak ill of the dead.'

That was a really odd thing for a widow to say, Ryan thought. As if her marriage hadn't really been that happy. There was something in her eyes...

But she'd closed the subject down. If he pushed now and asked her personal questions, then she might ask him personal questions, too; and he didn't want to talk about his past. About the wreck of his marriage. About the way he just couldn't connect with anyone.

They chatted about the hospital and Georgie's replacement car for a while, and then she yawned. 'Sorry. It must be all the country air making me so sleepy. I'll see you tomorrow,' she said.

When she left the room, Ryan sat on the sofa with Truffle sprawled over his lap. 'You like her, too, don't you?' he asked.

The dog licked his hand, as if to agree.

'But I hardly know her, and she has a real life four hundred miles south of here,' he said. 'And I'm not good at relationships. It wouldn't be fair to either of us if I started something. I'd make her miserable and...' He grimaced. 'Better to treat her as if she's just any other member of the team.'

And that was precisely what he did, the next day, when he did the ward rounds with Georgie and Alistair.

'As you've not been rostered together, you probably haven't met properly, yet, so I'll introduce you,' Ryan said. 'Georgie, this is Alistair, our F2 doctor—he's doing his final rotation with us. Al, this is Georgie—she's Clara's job swap partner.'

Once they'd done the social niceties, they started on the ward round. Ryan let Georgie lead, because he wanted to see how she worked.

He was pleased to notice she was great with the children and with any parents who happened to be visiting, greeting them warmly and listening to what the children said about how they were feeling. Before each patient, too, he noticed that she checked Alistair's knowledge of symptoms and treatments, and she let him take the lead on a couple of the more straightforward cases—just as Ryan would have done.

Warm, confident, capable and good at training. She was the perfect paediatric doctor, he thought. And then he had to suppress the thought that popped into his head about how she might be great with him, too. *Not* happening, he reminded himself.

After the ward round, Ryan worked with Alistair in clinic, but he'd made sure to invite Georgie and Parminder to lunch, too, to help Georgie get to know the team a bit better.

'So you don't like football or rugby?' Alistair asked Georgie over lunch.

'I don't like sport, full stop,' Georgie admitted. 'Watching or playing.'

Alistair looked aghast. 'How do you keep fit, then?'

'I make sure I walk ten thousand steps a day,' Georgie said, flashing the watch on her wrist, which doubled as a fitness tracker, 'and in London I did a Zumba class with my best friend.'

'I go to a Zumba class,' Parminder said. 'It's on Monday nights. Do you want to come with me next week?'

'Thanks, I'd love to,' Georgie said, smiling broadly.

'You could come training with me, too, if you like,' Alistair offered.

'Al, you big show-off, of course she doesn't want to train with *you*.' Parminder rolled her eyes. 'He does triathlons,' she told Georgie. 'That's just radge.'

'Radge?' Georgie asked, mystified.

'Crazy,' Ryan supplied. 'It's Edinburgh slang.'

'And Al is the living definition. Miles of running, miles of cycling, and then a freezing cold swim—for miles. Totally radge,' Parminder said.

'Ye've a lot to learn, hen,' Alistair said, hamming up the accent. 'Anyway, I'm not the only one with radge tendencies. There's Ryan tromping through the hills with his wee dawgeh even when it's stoating.'

'Stoating?' Georgie asked, wondering if her colleagues were making up words just to tease her, or if she was going to have to learn a whole new language up here.

'It's stoating when the rain's coming down so hard that it's bouncing back off the ground,' Alistair said.

'And remember this is the dog who chewed Clara's favourite shoes,' Parminder added. '*Three pairs* of them.'

'I replaced them all,' Ryan protested. 'Though it's not my fault if Clara leaves her shoes where Truffle can get them.'

'Just be warned, hen. That wee dog's not to be trusted,' Alistair said in a stage whisper. Then he smiled. 'So what else did you do for fun in London?'

'Music, theatre and history,' Georgie said promptly.

'Well, you're a wee bit late for the Fringe,'

Alistair said. 'But there are good theatres and music venues in the city.'

'And there's loads of history,' Parminder added. 'Have you been to the castle yet?'

'On my first morning here,' Georgie said with a smile, 'and I loved it.'

'And there's Mary King's Close—part of a seventeenth-century street that was buried when they built the Royal Exchange,' Alistair added. 'You might like that. If you don't mind the ghosts...'

Ryan groaned. 'Don't start on about non-existent things, Al.'

'He doesn't believe in Nessie, either, poor man,' Alistair confided to Georgie. 'No romance in his soul, that one.'

'Talking of romance, you have to visit Doune Castle,' Parminder said. 'I take it you've seen *Outlander*?'

'I love that series,' Georgie said. 'My best friend Sadie and I binge-watched it together. You can't get better than a gorgeous man in a kilt.'

A dark, brooding Scotsman. She couldn't help looking at Ryan, who was the epitome of a brooding Scotsman. He was sitting right opposite her. If she moved her foot, she'd be touching his: and the thought made her feel hot all over.

* * *

Georgie had going all pink and flustered—and yet again Ryan noticed how pretty she was. His libido seemed to have taken over his brain; he could imagine how *he* could make her all flustered, with little teasing kisses that would make her as hot and bothered as he felt right now.

Think of cool things, he told himself.

Going ankle deep into a hidden puddle.

Trudging across the hills with Truffle when the wind and the rain wouldn't let up.

And how soft Georgie's mouth was...

Oh, help. He really needed to get a grip.

'A kilt and a plaid.' Parminder fanned herself.

'Don't forget a jacket and cravat,' Georgie said.

'And boots,' Parminder added with a dramatic sigh.

'Gorgeous men in period costumes. Totally irresistible,' Georgie said.

Ryan had a kilt. Zoe had bought it for him years ago, to wear at a wedding. Why he'd even packed it when he'd left their house, he had no idea.

He shoved the thought away. He was *not* dressing up in a kilt to bowl Georgie over. They were colleagues. They were at work. *Focus,* he told himself.

Parminder laughed. 'Seriously, Georgie, Doune Castle is spectacular and so are the views. With or without a man in a kilt.'

'It's already on my list,' Georgie said with a smile. 'I was planning to go exploring a bit on my day off.'

So why, Ryan thought, did he have to mess it up by saying, 'Maybe I could drive you at the weekend and show you around the area a bit?'

Georgie's eyes widened. 'I can't ask you to give up your time off.'

Which was his cue to back off. But his mouth seemed to have other ideas. 'Dogs are allowed at some of the historic places, and Truffle's always up for a walk somewhere different. There's the beach, too.'

'Edinburgh has a beach?' Georgie looked surprised.

'Several. There's loads of golden sand at Portobello,' Parminder said.

Shut up, shut up, Ryan told himself. But the words came spilling out despite himself. 'Then maybe we could go to the seaside on Saturday and Doune Castle on Sunday—or whenever our off-duty coincides.'

'I'd like that,' she said, giving him a shy smile.

Oh, help. That smile made him feel even hotter. He needed to get the team involved before he really got out of control. 'I was thinking, we could do with a team night out.'

'If there's dancing, I'm so there. If only to laugh at Al's two left feet,' Parminder said with a grin.

'I'll teach you to dance, Al,' Georgie promised.

And how ridiculous was it that Ryan felt a huge twinge of jealousy?

'You'll be kind to me, hen, won't you?' Alistair asked, clearly trying his best to look piteous.

Ryan wasn't feeling particularly kind towards his colleague, right then. What did Alistair think he was doing, flirting with Georgie like that? 'It doesn't have to be dancing. We could go to an open mic night or something.'

'Dancing works for me,' Parminder said.

'Then can I delegate the organisation to you, Parm?' Ryan asked.

'Sure. I'll find us a ceilidh, so Georgie can go to a proper Scots dance,' Parminder said.

'That,' Georgie said, 'is a brilliant idea.'

'Thanks, Parm. Put the details on the team group chat when you've got them. And maybe we can do a pizza and bowling night or something before then to welcome Georgie to the team.'

'Yes, boss,' Parminder said with a grin.

* * *

This, Georgie thought, was the best day she'd had in Edinburgh so far: the first one where she was starting to feel part of the team, accepted for who she was. Nobody pitied her, the way they did in London. And it was all thanks to Ryan, who'd drawn her in to the group.

As for Ryan himself… She was just going to have to damp down the flares of attraction that kept threatening to overwhelm her.

Even if he was gorgeous.

Even if she could imagine him wearing a kilt and plaid, looking incredibly sexy.

Even if she did find herself wondering what it would feel like to dance with him…

Back at the cottage that evening, when Ryan came home from taking Truffle out, he took out his phone and flicked into his calendar. 'I'm off duty on Saturday and Sunday. What about you?'

'I'm off, too,' she said.

'Then we could go to the beach on Saturday and Doune on Sunday, if you like,' he said.

'It's not fair to make you give up your weekend to play tourist with me.'

'It's no bother. Truffle's always up for a walk somewhere different. We can't take her to Doune, but she loves the beach.'

* * *

The rest of the week flew by, and on Saturday morning it was unseasonably warm; Ryan drove them to Portobello straight after breakfast. Georgie loved all the Georgian buildings with bay windows and turrets; when they got to the beach itself, the tide was out and there were children making sandcastles, and people on paddle-boards.

Ryan crouched down by Truffle. 'I'm trusting you, mind,' he said. He ruffled the top of the dog's head, and let her off her lead. Georgie took her shoes off, enjoying the feel of the warm sand under her toes and the wind in her hair. It was ages since she'd been to the beach and she'd forgotten how much she liked the faint taste of salt in the air, the scent of the ocean and the sound of the waves swishing over the sand.

As they walked her hand brushed against Ryan's and for a nanosecond she actually thought about curling her fingers round his. What would it be like to walk barefoot on this beach with him at sunrise, hand in hand? Then maybe they'd stop and watch the changing colours of the sky, and turn to each other and kiss...

The urge to hold his hand grew stronger, but fear held her back. Supposing he rejected her? How awkward it would be. Then again, if he held her hand, that was an even more scary proposition: it would be the beginning of a relationship, and she'd have to take a leap and trust him. After Charlie, she wasn't sure she wanted to risk trusting again.

Truffle circled back to them at Ryan's whistle; she clearly loved the freedom of running around at the beach. Ryan took a Frisbee from his backpack. 'Fancy a game with me and Truffle?' he asked.

Keeping it light and not intense: that worked for her. 'Sure.'

It was the first time she'd seen Ryan look really relaxed, out here with the sun and the sand and his dog. He looked younger, more carefree; his grey eyes crinkled at the corners when he smiled, and he was so gorgeous that she found herself catching her breath. And when he caught her gaze, she felt seriously hot under the collar. She hadn't reacted to anyone like that since she was a teenager.

Right in the middle of their game, another dog came bounding past. Truffle dropped the Frisbee and took off after the other dog, clearly relishing a game of chase, and ignored Ryan completely when he called her name.

'Oh, no.' He took a box from the backpack and whistled. 'Truffle! Come here! Sausage!'

Truffle took no notice whatsoever, until the

other dog's owner called him back to heel. Only then did she seem to remember that she was supposed to be here with Ryan and Georgie and trotted back to them.

'What am I going to do with you?' Ryan asked, feeding her a bit of sausage. 'Well done for finally coming back. But we're going to have to work on recall again.' He glanced at Georgie, his eyes narrowing slightly. 'I'm not spoiling her, by the way. I'm rewarding her for doing what I asked, even though it took her a while. If I shouted at her, she'd associate coming back with being shouted at and that'd make her less likely to come when I call.'

She remembered what he'd said about Truffle being abandoned as a pup. Scaring her off was the last thing he'd want to do. 'Hey, I'm not judging. I know nothing about dog training.' She put her hand out to stroke the top of Truffle's head.

Again, her fingers brushed against his. And this time she noticed the slash of colour across his cheekbones. So did he feel this same wobbly sensation in the pit of his stomach? If so, what were they going to do about it?

'I'll just give Truffle a drink.' He took water and a bowl from his backpack.

Ryan McGregor was a man who truly took care of his own.

So unlike Charlie, who'd seemed so caring when they'd first got together but had turned out to be totally careless with her heart.

The more Georgie looked back on her marriage, the more she wondered how she'd missed all the clues. All the little things—like never making her a mug of coffee when he'd made one for himself—that she'd told herself to ignore because they just meant her husband had a tough day in the Emergency Department: maybe they hadn't been that at all. She'd let herself be blinded by his charm and hadn't seen the self-centred man behind it all. The man who'd lied to her, and who'd lied to his mistress. The man who'd let her down time after time, and she'd made excuses for him because she'd so wanted their marriage to work.

How could she trust her judgement any more?

'Are you OK?' Ryan asked, looking up at her when he'd put the empty bowl back in his backpack.

'Uh-huh,' she said.

'Sometimes you just need the sound of the sea to clear your head,' Ryan said, and she wondered what had made him feel that he needed his head cleared. His ex, maybe? Did he miss her?

She realised she'd spoked aloud when Ryan

said, 'I miss bits of Zoe. I miss the good times.' His eyes were unreadable. 'Do you miss Charlie?'

She had a choice: to keep living the lie she'd told in London, or to tell the truth and clear a way for herself to move forward, to finally get over her past. 'I miss him,' she said. Ryan's expression was still absolutely inscrutable. 'But, like you, I miss bits. The good bits.'

Which sounded as if there had been bad bits, too, Ryan thought. 'Sometime the bad stuff gets in the way and you don't mean to hurt each other,' he said.

'I don't think Charlie meant to hurt me. He just didn't consider me,' she said, looking bleak. 'I look back and I wonder if I fooled myself right from the start and saw the man I wanted him to be, not the man he really was. And I wanted my marriage to work, so I ignored things I maybe should've made a stand about.'

It sounded as if she'd been really struggling; as well as losing her husband she was facing up to the fact that her marriage hadn't been what she'd hoped it would be. And all the while people had been pitying the grieving widow. That was enough to mess with anyone's head.

'Sometimes you need space to think about what you really want,' he said. 'And the sea's good for that. I used to walk here when I was thinking about how things were with me and Zoe. Before I got Truffle.' When he'd seen the children playing on the beach, seen the families, and wondered what was so wrong with him that he couldn't give Zoe what she wanted.

'I'm hoping that distance will stop all the pity,' she said.

Which told him she didn't want him to pity her, either. If he offered her a hug, would she see it as pity? Or would she return that hug, hold him close?

And, if she held him close, what then? Where would it go? There was a lot more to her past than met the eye, and he didn't want to trample on a sore spot—or let her down, the way he'd let Zoe down.

So, even though he had an idea that she too felt that crazy spark whenever they accidentally touched, he didn't know how to deal with it.

'Sometimes you have to learn to leave the past behind,' he said. 'Try and get past the regrets and the might-have-beens. And then you can make the most of tomorrow.'

'When you've made mistakes, it's hard to trust yourself again,' she said, sounding so vulnerable that he wanted to wrap his arms around her and keep her safe.

But he hadn't kept Zoe's heart safe, so how

could he be sure that he'd keep Georgie's safe? What she'd just said… 'You're so right,' he agreed. 'I think all you can do is give it time.'

'I've already given it time. It's been more than a year, for me,' she said.

'Me, too.'

They were almost strangers, Maybe they'd be good for each other; maybe they wouldn't. But right here, right now, he wasn't risking it. 'Let's go and grab a coffee,' he said. 'There's a dog-friendly café up the road.' Somewhere with people close by so they wouldn't be so intimate.

The café was right on the edge of the beach, with a slate roof, dormer windows and a turret. Inside, it was all scrubbed wood tables, teamed with bentwood chairs; on the walls were fairy lights and framed old photographs.

'Cappuccino with no chocolate on top, right?' he asked.

Georgie was impressed that he'd noticed what she drank in the canteen at work. 'Thank you.'

The coffee turned out to be excellent. He held up his mug, saying, *'Slàinte mhath.'*

'Slanj-a-va?' she repeated.

He smiled. 'It's Gaelic for "Good health"— and that was a pretty good first attempt at pronouncing it. Anyway, to friendship.'

It was kind of a warning that he wasn't prepared to offer anything more. But she wasn't ready to risk her heart again, so she'd take that. 'To friendship,' she said.

The next morning, Ryan made a fuss of Truffle, promising to take her out later, before driving Georgie the hour to Doune Castle.

It had been a while since he'd last visited, but the building was spectacular: a fourteenth-century courtyard castle with a gatehouse that towered a hundred feet up, made of reddish-brown stone with white quoins.

'That's stunning,' Georgie said, looking awed. 'I mean, I've seen it on TV as the setting for several series, but I still didn't expect it to be this magnificent.'

Part of him wanted to reach out and take her hand—to walk hand in hand through the castle with her. But the idea made him feel edgy; there was so much that could go wrong. So he fell back on the safety of dry facts. 'It was built for Robert Stewart, the first Duke of Albany. It has one of the best-preserved halls in Scotland.'

He was really glad he'd checked his phone the night before and looked up facts and figures, because it meant he could talk to her about history instead of blurting out his feelings as they wandered through the castle.

'Look at that fireplace! It's taller than me, and it's massive. I can just imagine sitting here at a really long table with a trencher in front of me, with dishes of carved meats and flagons of ale,' she said as they walked through the Great Hall.'

He'd always thought that he didn't have much imagination, but suddenly he could see her sitting beside him in a wine-coloured velvet dress, her golden hair long and wavy and topped by a crown, and a choker of emeralds to match her eyes…

Spending time with Georgie made him feel different. It made him see his surroundings through fresh eyes; he'd grown so used to the hills and the sunrises and the sheep that he'd taken them for granted, but Georgie had made him look at things differently, really see them. The wide expanse of Porty Beach, the imposing ruins here, then clambering over the uneven path by the battlement to look out over the river to the Menteith Hills and Ben Lomond in the distance. How had he forgotten how amazing this was?

Then she tripped, and he grabbed her to keep her safe.

Oh, help. Being this close to her, feeling the warmth of her body against his—it made him want more.

She looked at him, and time seemed to stop. He was oh, so aware of how wide her eyes were, how soft her mouth was, how easy it would be to dip his head and kiss her.

He was at the point of doing exactly that when there was a cough beside them, followed by a plaintive, 'Do you mind letting us get past?'

Saved by the tourist, he thought as he dropped his arms from round Georgie and moved so the man and his family could get past.

'Are you OK?' he asked. Georgie looked shaken. Because of her near trip right next to the castle battlements and a sheer drop, or because of the almost-kiss? He was too scared of the answer to ask.

'I'm fine,' she said, sounding a little breathless. 'Thank you for stopping me falling.'

'You're welcome,' he said, but he was still tingling all over from touching her.

Once they were back on the ground floor, they wandered through the gift shop, and Georgie seemed highly amused by the basket of coconut shells for visitors to borrow—and the children running round in the courtyard outside, banging the coconut shells together and pretending to be horses.

'I still can't quite get over the fact that I'm

walking round the Monty Python castle. It's my dad's favourite film. Would you mind taking a snap of me on my phone in front of the castle, so I can print it off and send it to him with some of those coconut shells?'

'Sure,' he said. And her delight in doing something nice for her dad made him feel as if something had cracked in the region of his heart. What would it be like to have that sort of bond with your family, that sort of closeness, all those shared memories? He wasn't envious, exactly; more wistful.

If his mum hadn't been killed, his life would've been so different. Maybe she would've made it up with her family; maybe she would've found a new partner and he would've had a dad, or even a baby brother or sister.

Nobody had loved him enough to want to keep him for long. Then again, he'd had the chance to make a family with Zoe, and he hadn't let his heart open wide enough to embrace a family. So really it was just as much his fault. What was wrong with him, that he couldn't let people close? Why was he so scared of rejection? Why couldn't he move on, away from his past?

He pushed the thoughts away and concentrated on her, taking the photograph as she'd asked.

'You could act a bit out in front of the curtain wall and I'll film it,' he said. 'Then you can send it to him after you've posted the shells to him.'

She laughed. 'Genius. Thank you.'

It was impossible not to laugh as she recreated a bit of the film.

'Did you ever think about acting?' he asked.

'No. I always wanted to be a doctor. And it wasn't just to copy my big brother—I wanted to make a difference and really help people,' she said. 'When I did my rotation, I was quite tempted by obstetrics, because I love those first precious moments of a new life. But I love working with children.'

Was it just working with kids, though? Was her biological clock ticking? He'd decided a long time ago that he didn't want kids. If Georgie did, then that was a good reason to keep things strictly platonic between them—otherwise he'd be letting her down, the same way he'd let Zoe down.

At the same time, the more time he spent with her, the more time he wanted to spend with her. She made him see the world in a different way.

She was here for six months. She wasn't necessarily looking for for ever. Maybe—the base of his spine tingled with longing—maybe they could have a fling. Be each other's transition person. Get this thing out of both of their systems and move on.

'What about you?' she asked.

'I wanted to make a difference, too.' Though he wasn't going to tell her that he'd wanted to help all the children who didn't have anyone else. That was too personal.

'We're on the same side, then,' she said. 'Right—giddy up.' She clicked her tongue and made the coconut shells sound like horses' hooves. 'Come on. You, too.'

How could he resist?

It was utterly ridiculous, pretending to be on horseback and galloping all the way back to the car. He probably looked like a total idiot. But Georgie was laughing and enjoying herself, and he realised that this was *fun*. He couldn't remember the last time he'd done anything like this, if ever.

Her eyes crinkled at the corners as she smiled at him. And it made his stomach swoop.

Once they were back the cottage, he took Truffle out on a long walk. Georgie joined them, but when they got back to the cottage he noticed how wet her feet were.

'Tomorrow,' he said, 'we need to get you some proper walking boots.'

'I'm on an early shift,' she said, 'and tomorrow night I'm going to Zumba with Parm.'

'We'll nip out in our lunch break, then,' he suggested. 'And Truffle agrees, don't you?'

The dog woofed softly. 'So that's settled, then,' he said with a smile.

CHAPTER FIVE

On Monday lunchtime, Georgie met Ryan in his office and they grabbed a sandwich on the way down to the city to choose some walking boots.

To her surprise, the man in the shop actually measured her feet, got her to try on three different pairs of boots along with thick, comfortable socks, and them asked her to climb over a 'bridge' in the middle of the shop that had an uneven rocky surface before bunny-hopping down a slope to see if the boots fitted properly.

This was definitely not something she'd ever done in London.

She wasn't used to wearing something close-fitting around her ankles and it felt weird; but, if it meant her feet stayed dry when she went out on the hills with Ryan and Truffle, she could put up with it.

'You need to wear them indoors for a couple of hours a night for the next week,' the shop assistant said when she'd chosen them, 'and if they're not comfortable just bring them back and tell us what you don't like about them, and we can find something that suits you better.'

'Thank you,' she said with a smile.

'And make sure you keep them out of Truffle's reach,' Ryan added.

After their shift, Ryan went home to walk the dog while Georgie went out to the Zumba class with Parminder.

'I'm so pleased you asked me to join you,' Georgie said.

'You're welcome. It's not easy to fit into a new department. And everyone loved Clara. It was a bit of a shock when she told us she was moving to London for six months and you were coming here in her place,' Parminder said. 'We had no idea she was so unhappy here.'

'Sometimes it's not so much being unhappy, more that you need a change so you can move forward from a situation,' Georgie said. 'She spoke really highly of everyone in the department. It wasn't anything that any of you did or didn't do.'

'Thanks. Because I just kept thinking that I must've been such a rubbish friend to her, and I feel bad about that. I won't push you to tell me anything you don't want to, though anything you do say to me I'll keep confidential,' Parminder said.

'Thanks,' Georgie said, appreciating the overture of friendship but not wanting to go back to the same problems she'd faced in London. Parminder would be kind, but Georgie didn't want to fight off another deluge of pity. She wanted to be *herself.* 'I just needed a change from London. Let's just say my personal life was a bit...' She wrinkled her nose. How did you describe becoming a widow and then discovering that the husband you'd thought was devoted was actually a cheat and a liar? 'Tricky.'

'Fair enough.' Parminder smiled. 'And at least Ryan's a nice housemate.'

'He's been kind,' Georgie said. At least, after the first couple of rocky days.

'I always used to think that he and Clara would get together after his marriage broke up,' Parminder said. 'But they're more like brother and sister. Clara said she loves him to bits as a friend, but there's just no chemistry between them and she doesn't fancy him.'

Whereas whenever Georgie let her mind wander she found herself thinking about Ryan McGregor. About how beautiful his mouth was. About how her skin tingled every time she was walking somewhere with him and her hand accidentally brushed his. About what it would be like to kiss him—especially since that moment at Doune when he'd stopped her falling and his arms had been wrapped round her, keeping her safe. If that tourist hadn't broken the moment, would he have kissed her? Would she have kissed him back?

'He's such a nice guy. But he's been so quiet since the divorce,' Parminder said. 'I think we all wish we could wave a magic wand and find the perfect partner for him.'

A perfect partner rules me out, Georgie thought. She obviously hadn't been enough for Charlie, or her husband wouldn't have had to find someone else to give him whatever had been lacking in their marriage. And Charlie was the only child of parents who loved him dearly; he'd never had to deal with heartbreak or misery. If she hadn't been enough to keep *him* happy, how could she possibly be enough for a man whose heart was already broken? Plus she was far from perfect.

She changed the subject quickly. 'It's the first time I've shared a house with a dog, too. I live on my own in London. Though my brother lives a couple of floors up in the same building. Our great-aunt left us both money, and we were lucky enough to get the chance to buy the flats when the building had just been renovated. Our parents had just retired and decided to move out of London, so it was kind of nice to still have family really close by.'

'I know what you mean,' Parminder said. 'Mine drive me crazy, sometimes, but it's good to know they're all close by.'

Ryan, Georgie thought, hadn't mentioned having family close by, even though he'd said he'd trained in Edinburgh. Though asking would be intrusive, and she didn't want to gossip about him.

Thankfully the class started then, and there wasn't time to chat any more.

On Thursday, Georgie had another case that puzzled her and led her to seek Ryan's advice.

'Run me through it,' he said.

'Ben's three. He has a fever, a rash and a swollen gland in his neck; the whites of his eyes are red and swollen, and he's got a sore throat. His mum says the family's new kitten scratched him on the face a few days ago and she thinks the scratch might be infected.'

'What do you think?' Ryan asked.

'I don't think it's anything to do with the scratch.' She frowned. 'The rash makes me think it could be scarlet fever, measles or possibly lupus. The swollen glands hint at glandular fever, or it might be the beginning of juvenile rheumatoid arthritis.'

'But?'

She grimaced. 'I've admitted him and put him on antibiotics. But his urine sample and white blood count don't show anything out of the ordinary, he's not responding to the usual treatment and his fever's spiking. I'm missing something. Would you have a look at him for me, please?'

'Of course.'

Georgie introduced Ryan to Ben and his mum. 'Ryan's going to take a second look at Ben for me, because Ben's test results aren't showing what I was expecting,' she said with a smile.

Ryan gently examined Ben, getting him to stick his tongue out. 'See how red his tongue is?' he said to Georgie and Ben's mum. 'And there are vertical cracks on his lips. The skin on his palms is a bit red, too. I think he has Kawasaki disease.'

'I've never heard of that,' Ben's mum said.

'It's quite rare,' Ryan said. 'It's also called mucocutaneous lymph node syndrome. Basically it's a disease where the blood vessels are inflamed, and we don't know what causes it—it might be an infection—but it's not contagious, and we can treat it.'

'With aspirin,' Georgie said, 'and immuno-globulin.'

'I thought you weren't supposed to give aspirin to children under the age of ten?' Ben's mum asked.

'Sixteen,' Ben said. 'You're right, because it can cause Reye's syndrome, but this is one of the very few medical cases where the best treatment for an under-sixteen is aspirin.'

'You might find the skin on Ben's hands peels a bit, over the next few days,' Georgie said, 'but it's nothing to worry about.' But she ordered an ECG and an echo to check Ben's heart, because she knew that one of the complications of Kawasaki disease was swollen and inflamed coronary arteries. To her relief, the tests showed that Ben was fine; and, the next day, his fever had broken.

That evening, there was a team night out of bowling and pizza. And how good it was to feel part of them, Georgie thought. Everyone seemed to see her for who she was: the London doctor who really wasn't into football or rugby, but who made good brownies. Best of all, nobody saw her as 'Poor Georgie'. They teased her about her accent and she was pretty sure there was a competition between her colleagues as to who'd be the first to flummox her with a new dialect word every day, but she felt that they'd accepted her. Including Ryan.

Though it didn't help that Ryan was on her bowling team, and she was sitting right next to him. There wasn't much room on the benches by their alley, so her thigh was pressed very closely against his. Despite the fact they were both wearing jeans, she was very aware of the warmth of his body. And, a couple of times when she glanced at him, he was looking at her, too. She thought back to that moment at Doune when he'd held her, when they'd been so close to kissing, and her heart skipped a beat. She was pretty sure he felt the same attraction that she did; but what were they going to do about it?

And if they did end up kissing, what then? She didn't want to make another mistake like she'd made with Charlie. And if she got this wrong, things could be very awkward between them at work and at the cottage. Maybe it was better to play safe. So she made sure she was sitting at the opposite end of the table when it came to the pizza part of the evening.

On the Monday evening, Georgie practically bounced into the cottage after her late shift; she'd been quiet for the last few days, so Ryan had been trying to work out how to ask her if he'd upset her. Maybe it hadn't been him at all; maybe it was something to do with her late husband.

'Hi. I'll just heat your stew through,' Ryan said. 'And there's a jacket potato.'

'Thank you. That's wonderful.'

'You look pleased,' he said.

'I am. Ben's definitely on the mend,' she said, accepting the bowlful of stew gratefully. 'And there are clear skies tonight.'

'That's great to hear about Ben, but I don't get what the fuss is about a clear sky tonight.' Ryan said.

'There's a meteor shower tonight, and it'll be amazing because out here it's practically pitch black skies.' Her eyes sparkled. 'Come and watch them with me when I've finished dinner.'

Standing with her under the stars.

Part of Ryan thought this was a dangerous move: he was already finding himself thinking about her at odd moments of the day. But part of him couldn't resist the idea of being close to her—even if she was only offering friendship. 'OK.'

After her meal, they went out to the garden.

'I love the stars out here,' she said. 'I never get to see them so well in London because there's too much light from the city.'

'So you're a star-gazing fan?'

She nodded. 'I've always wanted to see the Northern Lights. I'd just about talked Charlie into agreeing to go on holiday to Finland, to stay in one of those hotels where the rooms have a glass ceiling so you can watch the sky as you fall asleep and hopefully see the Northern Lights.' She shrugged. 'But then he was killed. And going on my own, or even with a friend, wouldn't have been the same.'

That gave him pause for thought. A couple of times now she'd hinted that her marriage hadn't been completely great. But what she'd just said: did it mean Charlie was the love of her life and she was still broken-hearted over his death? 'I'm sorry,' he said awkwardly.

'Thank you.'

She looked embarrassed, and he wished he hadn't been so clumsy. 'There's a good chance you'll see the lights while you're up here.'

'Wouldn't I have to go to the Orkneys or something, to be far north enough?' she asked.

'No, they've been seen here in Edinburgh.'

'Maybe I'll get Dad to forward his text alerts to me, then,' she said. 'Oh! Look up!'

He followed where she was pointing, and saw a meteor streaking across the sky.

'That's beautiful,' he said. 'I get why you

like the night sky. I've never actually noticed a meteor before.'

'They're not hugely common, except when there's a big shower, and then if the moon's bright you might not actually see that many.' She smiled. 'You're supposed to wish on a falling star.'

What would he wish for?

A magic wand, perhaps, to fix things for people when they went wrong.

Or maybe to fix the broken parts of himself, so he actually had something to offer someone. So he'd be able to let a partner close instead of keeping those last barriers round his heart, scared that if he let her closer she'd find him wanting and walk away—just as everyone in his life had since his mother's death, except his dog.

Truffle didn't expect him to talk about feelings; she was happy just to be with him, to walk with him on the beach or over the hills, and curl up by the fire with him. She accepted him for what he was. Whereas a relationship meant talking and sharing feelings, letting someone see deeper into him and risking that they wouldn't want what they saw.

'What would you wish for?' he asked, to distract himself.

'Ah, no. Telling what you wish for means it won't come true.'

What would she wish for? Obviously to have Charlie back, for him not to have died.

But if by any chance her wish was to fall in love again, could it be with him? Could they find some way to make this work? He had no idea.

But here, with the meteors streaking across the sky, he was starting to think there were possibilities. That maybe they could help each other over their pasts, step by tiny step. He just had to find the right way to suggest it.

Over the new few days, Georgie really felt that she was settling in and enjoying everything Edinburgh had to offer, from the theatre to the pandas at the zoo; and she found herself enjoying the fact that Hayloft Cottage was in the middle of nowhere. She liked getting up and seeing the sheep from next door peering in through the kitchen window; she liked sharing her space with a dog who'd grown used to her enough to curl up on the sofa next to her when she sat reading a magazine, with her chin resting on Georgie's knees; and she liked the feeling of freshness and hearing the birds sing when she walked out of the front door in the morning.

She enjoyed the hospital, too—and she was glad that Ryan was on with her in the PAU when a mum came in, panicking. 'My baby! He's all floppy and he keeps being sick and I can't get to see my family doctor and…'

'It's OK,' Georgie reassured her. 'You're in the right place.'

Ryan took the baby and started to examine him, while Georgie tried to ascertain the medical history. 'Tell us about your little boy.'

'Max is four months. He's never been a good feeder, and my milk's drying up so I've been giving him a few bottles to keep him going,' Max's mum said. 'I thought he'd picked up a bug, because he's been sick and had diarrhoea for the last couple of days, but then this morning I noticed this rash, and he was wheezing, and he's floppy—and all the baby books say if he's floppy it's really serious, and… Please, just help him,' she begged.

Georgie was pretty sure she'd seen cases like this before in London. 'So you're giving him formula as well as breastfeeding? Has he been sick before when you gave him formula?'

'He was sick on the breast, too,' Max's mum said. 'Do you think it's the formula that's made him worse?'

'I think there's a strong possibility he might have a milk allergy,' Georgie said. 'And that's not just the formula—if you've had any dairy, that will go through your breast milk. Are there any allergies in your family, or does anyone have asthma or hay fever?'

'Nothing like that.' Max's mum looked worried.

'I'd like to do a blood test to check my diagnosis,' Georgie said.

'I think she's right,' Ryan said. 'Have you seen any blood or mucus in Max's stools, when they've been solid?'

'Yes. I was so scared it was cancer or something like that.'

'I'm pretty sure it's a milk allergy,' Georgie said again. 'That would explain why he's not feeding well, too. Once we get that sorted out, you'll find he gains weight well and you'll be a lot less worried about him.'

Max's mum bit her lip. 'If he's allergic to formula, what am I going to do? Give him soy?'

'Often there's an allergy to soy as well,' Georgie said. 'We can give you a hypoallergenic formula to try.'

'And a calcium supplement,' Ryan added, 'and a multivitamin syrup with vitamin D.'

'Let me sort out the blood test,' Georgie said. 'We'll see how Max goes on the hypoallergenic formula, and then bring him in to reintroduce a milk feed and see if he reacts. We'll do the test here, so if he reacts strongly we can help straight away. And if we're right you'll need to check the labels for absolutely everything you feed him, to make sure you avoid giving him anything with milk in it for at least the first year.'

'About one in five babies outgrow a milk allergy by the time they're a year old,' Ryan said, 'and most have outgrown it by the time they're three, but some will have an immediate reaction to even small traces of dairy.'

Georgie cleaned Max's heel and took a tiny sample of blood through a heel prick test. 'It's only temporarily uncomfortable,' she reassured Max's mum. 'It'll take a couple of days to get the results back, but in the meantime we'll sort out the formula for you.

'So he's going to be all right?' she asked.

Georgie rested her hand on the woman's shoulder. 'Yes. I know right now everything looks scary, but Dr McGregor and I have seen a lot of poorly babies in our time, and we've made them better. There are lots of things we can do to help Max.'

That was one of the things Ryan really liked about Georgie: she was calm, kind and practical. While she talked to Max's mum about how to read labels and what kind of alternatives to try when weaning, Max's mum was visibly relaxing and seeming more confident in her ability to manage.

Funny, Georgie made him feel that way, too. Not so much in his job—he knew what he was doing at the hospital—but outside. When he was with her, he saw the world in a different way. He was starting to feel *connected*. It scared him, because he'd never managed to do that before; yet at the same time he wanted more. Much more.

The following night, Georgie was woken by an insistent knocking on her bedroom door.

She grabbed her dressing gown, wrapped it round her and stomped over to the door. 'What?' she snapped as she opened the door to Ryan.

'You need to come outside,' he said. 'Right now.'

'I was asleep and I'm in my pyjamas,' she pointed out, glaring at him.

'Just get your coat and your boots on. Now. You'll really regret it if you don't.'

'Are you insane?' She glanced at her watch. 'It's one in the morning and I'm on an early.'

'I know. Stop arguing, Georgie. It's important.'

Important? How? If it was a fire, she would've

heard the smoke alarm. Why was he looking so pleased with himself? Why wasn't he explaining whatever it was? Why was he such an irritating man?

He waited for her to walk before him, not leaving her with much choice.

Scowling, she pulled her boots and her coat on, and followed him out to the garden.

'Look up,' he said.

She did so, and felt her eyes widen as she realised why he'd wanted her to go outside—and why he hadn't explained. He'd wanted this to be a surprise. A delight.

And it was.

Above them, curtains of pale green light rippled slowly across the sky, the stars still visible through the green haze. The thing she'd always wanted to see. *The Northern Lights.*

She'd never seen anything so gorgeous and breathtaking before.

'Oh, my God, Ryan, it's…' Words failed her, and she stood staring up at the sky, utterly entranced.

She had no idea quite how it happened, but then his arm was wrapped round her shoulders and hers was round his waist.

It was just for bodily warmth, she told herself, because it was a cold night and they had pyjamas on under their coats.

And when he stooped slightly so his cheek was against hers, again she told herself it was just for warmth.

But then somehow they ended up facing each other. He rested his palm against her cheek, and she found herself doing the same. Right here, right now, under the glow of the Northern Lights, everything felt like a different world. A magical one, full of possibilities.

He dipped his head, and brushed his mouth very lightly against hers. Her lips tingled at the touch: an invitation, a promise, a temptation. Warmth and sweetness. A real connection. Things that had been missing from her life for so very long.

And she couldn't help responding, sliding her hand round to the back of his head and urging his mouth down to hers again. His kiss was long and slow, and so very sweet that it made her ache. Asking, not demanding; it made her feel as if she was unfurling under the spring sunshine after a hard and lonely winter, as if the dancing lights in the sky were flickering inside her head, and she didn't want it to stop.

Yet, at the same time, common sense seeped back into her along with the chill of the night air.

She was kissing her housemate.

Ryan was gorgeous, but he'd had a miserable time in the past. And how did she know things would even work between them? Hadn't she learned the hard way through Charlie that her judgement in men wasn't good enough?

She pulled away. 'This isn't a good idea.'

His eyes were dark and unreadable. She didn't have a clue what was going on in his head.

But then he nodded. 'You're right. We'll forget this ever happened. Blame it on the excitement of seeing the Northern Lights.'

Lights that even now were fading away, melting back into the stratosphere.

Just like that feeling of warmth and connection.

Leaving her back in the shadows of loneliness.

'Agreed,' she said, trying to stem the sudden flood of misery.

It was only a kiss.

A temporary aberration.

Not to be repeated.

'Thank you for waking me to see the lights,' she said, putting as much politeness as she could into her voice. Distance, that was what she needed most right now. 'See you tomorrow.'

'Yeah,' he said, and let her walk back into the house without following her.

* * *

What the hell had he been thinking?

Of course it wasn't a good idea to kiss her.

Ryan knew he'd come up with a pathetic excuse. Blame it on the Northern Lights, indeed. He knew precisely why he'd kissed Georgie. She'd switched from super-grouchy at being woken in the middle of the night to almost glowing with joy when she'd seen the display of lights dancing through the skies. He'd found her delight irresistible, to the point where his common sense had been completely bypassed by need and he'd held her close. She'd held him back. And then he'd kissed her, her mouth warm and soft and sweet under his. She'd kissed him back. He'd felt the kind of connection he hadn't thought was possible for him.

And then she'd stopped kissing him and said it wasn't a good idea.

She was right. Of course it wasn't a good idea. It was stupid. She was still mourning her husband, Ryan wasn't a good bet when it came to relationships, and they were only going to be in each other's lives temporarily.

Utterly stupid.

But what was even more stupid was that he wouldn't have changed a thing. If he could rewind time and go back to the second when he'd slid his arm round her shoulders... He would still have done it. He would still have touched her face like that. Still have kissed her.

And he'd lied—to both of them—when he'd said that they could just forget it had ever happened. Because he couldn't forget it. That kiss just kept replaying in his head, in full Technicolor. When Ryan finally went to bed, he dreamed about kissing Georgie. He woke, aching, because he wasn't kissing her; and then he thought about it all over again. Drifted back into a fitful doze. Dreamed again. Woke again, thinking of her.

What had the actor said in that Shakespeare play Zoe had taken him to, a couple of years back, the one with the magician standing on the top of the stage with his cloak billowing out like a stormy sky as he conjured up a tempest?

When I wak'd, I cried to dream again...

But dreams could be broken all too easily.

Giving up on sleep, Ryan went out for a long walk with Truffle. Thank God he and Georgie were on different shifts today. She'd be gone by the time he got back to the cottage, and he could have a cold shower—and hopefully some common sense would leach back into his head along with the water.

And then somehow he'd have to find his way back to a decent working relationship with her.

CHAPTER SIX

OVER THE NEXT few days, Georgie was pretty sure that Ryan was avoiding her. And it was her own fault, for kissing him. She shouldn't have done it. When he'd slipped his arm round her shoulders, she should've found an excuse to step away, instead of leaning into him and sliding her arm round his waist. She should never have responded.

'How am I going to convince him that it was a mistake and I'm not going to make life difficult for him?' she asked Truffle.

The dog just gave a soft wuff, as if to say that she didn't have a clue, either.

It was fine until the Friday morning. And then she made the mistake of flicking into her social media account and all the memories popped up from six years ago. Her wedding day. Pictures of herself and Charlie in the doorway of the tiny ancient church where they'd just pledged to love, honour and cherish each other.

Forsaking all others.

Had he meant it at the time?

She'd loved him so much. She'd thought they were so good together. They'd got on well with each other's families, they'd got on well with each other's friends, their jobs had complemented each other's, and that day had been so bright and sparkly. The sun had shone all day, and she'd thought they were so lucky to spend such a perfect day with their family and their closest friends, sharing the love and the hope and the joy. She'd graduated and had been halfway through her foundation training, whereas Charlie was two years older and working in the Accident and Emergency Department.

They'd had such plans.

She'd finish her training, do three years in her specialty, and then they'd think about starting a family.

Except Charlie had found a reason to put off having children with her: a reason Georgie had had no idea about at the time. Trisha Hampson, the woman he'd had an affair with. A long-running affair that had started a good year before he'd died and had then continued through every disaster mission he'd gone to help with.

And, just before that last mission, according to what Trisha's parents had told her later, Trisha had found out that she was pregnant.

Had she told Charlie straight away? Or had she wanted to wait until she could tell him face to face, and maybe they'd both been killed before she'd had a chance to tell him?

If they hadn't been killed in the landslide, would he have told Georgie about Trisha and the baby when he came back to England? Would he have chosen to stay with her and give Trisha financial support for the baby, or would he have left Georgie and gone to live with his new family?

And why had he needed to have that affair in the first place? Hadn't she made him happy? She'd never had any real fights with him, and she'd always agreed to whatever he wanted. She'd thought they were good together. What had been missing, for him, in their relationship? Where had she gone wrong?

All that potential, all that sparkle on their wedding day: now she looked at the photographs, and the day just felt tarnished. Her marriage had been a big, fat lie, and she'd been too stupid to realise it until it was too late.

She wasn't even aware she was crying until the kitchen door opened and Ryan walked in with Truffle.

'Georgie? What's wrong?' he asked.

'Nothing.' She rubbed her eyes with the back of her hand.

'It doesn't look like nothing.' He filled the kettle and switched it on. 'I prescribe a mug of tea. And I'm…' He paused. 'I'm not prying, but I'm here if you want to talk about it—and it won't be going any further than me.'

Nobody at St Christopher's knew that she was a widow. He'd kept his promise about that. She really had to stop letting Charlie's behaviour affect every other relationship she had. Just because he'd been a cheat and a liar, it didn't follow that everyone else in the world was, too.

'It's my wedding anniversary,' she admitted. 'Or it would have been.' Would she even still have been married? Charlie's child would've been crawling by now.

'It's the first anniversary since he died?'

'Second,' she said. The first one, though, she hadn't known about Trisha, and she'd still been mourning the man she'd thought she'd married. Now… It was different. She knew Charlie hadn't loved her as much as she'd loved him, or he wouldn't have had the affair.

Ryan clearly thought she was still in mourning; maybe that was why he'd backed off so fast after their kiss. Should she tell him the truth? But then he really might be tempted to pity her—not just poor, widowed Georgie, but poor, widowed, clueless, cheated-on Georgie. She didn't want that.

* * *

Georgie looked totally lost, and Ryan had to stop himself walking over and putting his arms round her. Things were still slightly awkward between them since he'd kissed her in the garden, and the last thing he wanted to do was make that awkwardness any worse.

'The photos came up on social media as a memory from six years ago. I should've expected it, but it caught me a bit on the raw.'

'I'm not pitying you,' he said softly, mindful of when she'd told him that her husband had been killed in a landslide while helping people after an earthquake. 'Of course something like this would catch you out. I'm planning to take Truffle for a very long walk by the sea on my wedding anniversary.' It would be the second anniversary for him, too, since the divorce.

'Do you miss her?' she asked.

'Sometimes,' he said. He didn't miss not living up to Zoe's expectations—or his own. 'I wish it could've worked out, but we wanted different things.' She'd wanted a baby. He hadn't. Not that he wanted to go into that. He shrugged. 'She was in PR. We were both busy with our careers and worked ridiculous hours. I guess we grew apart.' That was true: just not the whole truth. 'It was an amicable split, or as amicable as it could be.' After the fights. When they'd sat down and finally been completely honest with each other. When they'd realised that their differences were irreconcilable.

But it had still hurt that Zoe had fallen for someone else so quickly. Someone who'd been prepared to give her the baby she wanted. He was glad that Zoe was happy again; but he hadn't really moved on and found someone else. Not because he still loved Zoe, but because he didn't want to risk letting someone else down, the way he'd let his wife down. And Georgie had already had too much loss in her life. She didn't need him complicating things for her.

'Things are as they are,' he said. 'I love my job, I love my dog, and I love Edinburgh.'

'You grew up here, didn't you?' she asked.

'Yes.'

'I miss my family,' she said.

Oh, no. Please don't let her ask him about his family. Because he didn't have one. Just a grave he visited on the anniversary of his mum's death. She'd been gone for three decades now; he had a couple of creased photographs of her that had survived the years of foster care, and that was it. 'You're welcome to invite them here. I could sleep on the couch.'

Her eyes glittered with tears. 'That's really kind of you, but I can't ask you to do that.'

'It's no bother. Besides, I wouldn't ask a guest to sleep down here with Truffle. She snores. And she's not above waking you in the middle of the night—that's why Clara bought the stair gate, after too many three a.m. visits from a dog who's bright enough to know how to open a door and will lick your nose until you wake up and give in to her demands for a walk.'

Truffle's tail thudded against the floor at the W-word, and he reached down to scratch behind her ears. 'Yes, you daft beastie, I'm talking about you.'

'I'm fine,' Georgie said. 'I guess…it just caught me a bit unawares.'

'Things do,' he said, feeling awkward.

'I never thought I'd be a widow at thirty. I thought I'd be a mum. I was so looking forward to having a family.'

And here it was. The same issue he'd faced with Zoe. Georgie, too, wanted to be a mum. Ryan hadn't wanted to be a dad. He knew nothing about *how* to be a dad. He'd never had a role model. His mum, until he was six; and then a string of foster parents who'd given up on him.

The one person who'd made a difference was the woman who'd come out of retirement to give temporary cover while his social worker had been on maternity leave: Elspeth Mc-Creadie. She'd sat down with his sulking teenage self and told him that life wasn't fair, and nobody pretended it was.

But he had a choice. He could focus on his past and be miserable for the rest of his life, or he could try making a difference to the world instead. That he was bright enough to do anything he wanted. He was good at science, so he could be a doctor, make other people better—and if he learned some social skills then his future could be better than his past. But Ryan was the only one who could make that difference to his own life. Nobody else would do it for him.

He'd been furious at the time, but her words had sunk in. He'd kept his supermarket checkout job at evenings and weekends, but he'd done his A levels and been accepted at university. Become a doctor. Made that difference to his own life. He'd stayed in touch with Elspeth, and although she'd died before his graduation she'd left him a congratulations card and written that she thought he could change the world and she was proud of him.

He still hadn't completely connected with anyone, though. He'd tried so hard to love Zoe the way she wanted to be loved; despite all the effort, he'd failed.

Fixing patients, he could do.

Emotional stuff...that was another matter. He didn't have the skill set.

'I'm sorry,' he said awkwardly, wanting to help but not knowing how.

She scrubbed a hand across her face. 'You can't always get what you want. I have a lot to be thankful for. I have my family, a job I love, good friends. I don't have to worry about whether I can pay the rent or afford to eat. Wanting more's just greedy.'

'Sometimes we all want more,' he said. 'Um, I'll make you a coffee.'

'It's fine. I need to get to work.'

A safe place, where she wouldn't have to think about her anniversary because she'd be busy helping patients. It was how he'd used work too ever since he and Zoe had split up.

'I'll see you later,' he said.

But she was quiet all weekend. And every time Ryan thought about giving her a hug, he remembered her words. *I never thought I'd be a widow at thirty. I thought I'd be a mum.*

He wanted her, but he didn't want to let her down. How could he get this to work? But, every time he thought about it, he came up blank.

On Wednesday, Georgie had the day off. She spent the morning cleaning, then nipped down to the farm shop to buy bread and stayed chatting with Janie for a bit. But, when she got back to the cottage, the patter of paws and waggy tail she was used to was missing.

'Truffle?' she called.

The house was silent.

Ryan was on an early shift. No way would he have come home halfway through it and taken Truffle out. So where on earth was the dog?

The stair gate was in place, so it wasn't likely the Labrador had gone upstairs.

And then she heard a creak.

The back door was open. Obviously she hadn't shut it properly and Truffle had gone into the garden. Except, when she looked outside, the dog wasn't there. 'Truffle,' she called. 'Here, girl.'

Nothing.

And there was a pile of dirt by the corner of the fence, along with a hole big enough for a large dog to squeeze through...

Oh, no. No, no, *no*.

It looked as if the dog had dug her way out of the garden. Ryan had said she was an absconder, and here was the proof.

'Truffle!' she yelled, hoping that she was wrong and the dog would appear from round the corner.

Still no response.

How did you get a dog to come back? When Truffle had disappeared to play with another dog on the beach, Ryan had given her slices of cocktail sausage when she'd come back.

OK. Sausage it was. Georgie ran to the fridge and took out Ryan's box of treats. 'Truffle,' she called. 'Sausage!' She rattled the box, and then opened it on the grounds that dogs had a brilliant sense of smell and Truffle would know there were treats on offer and come to get them.

But the dog didn't appear.

Oh, God. *She'd lost Ryan's dog.* She didn't even know where to begin looking for Truffle. And she didn't know the countryside around here well enough to know where the dog might have been most likely to head for. Panicking, she called the ward.

'Is Ryan there, please?' she asked. 'It's an emergency.'

What seemed like ten years later, Ryan came to the phone. 'What's the emergency?' he asked.

'It's Truffle. I went down to Janie's and I must've not shut the back door properly. There's a hole by the fence and I think she's tunnelled out of the garden. I can't see her anywhere and

I've called and called and I've offered sausage and—'

'Stop gabbling and breathe,' he cut in. 'You're quite sure she's not there?'

'I'm sure. Where do I start looking for her?'

'You don't,' he said. 'Stay where you are and I'll go and find her.' He banged the phone down.

This was all her fault. And if the dog was hurt, or had been hit by a car and was...

Oh, God. She cut the thought off, feeling sick to her stomach. If Truffle was injured or worse, she'd never forgive herself.

Not knowing what to do, but feeling that she had to do something, she put her phone on charge, put the kettle on to make a flask of coffee and stuffed a first aid kit and a towel into a waterproof bag, together with a torch and a bottle of water and the box of sausage slices. Then she laced up her hiking boots and got her coat ready.

Ryan was back at the cottage sooner than she'd expected, which told her that he must've broken the speed limit all the way back from the city.

'Ryan, I'm s—' she began.

'Save it. I need to find my dog.' His face was a mask of suppressed anger and worry.

'I'll go with you. I've got a bag. A towel, first aid kit, coffee, water. My phone.'

'Half the time there isn't a signal out there.'

'I'm sorry. I'll—'

'Save it,' he said again.

'Look, I know you're furious with me and don't want me around, and I hate myself for being so careless with her, but two pairs of eyes are better than one when you're looking,' she said. 'I can't just stay here doing nothing. Let me come with you.'

He scowled at her; but then, to her relief, he nodded.

Please let Truffle be all right.

Please let her not be badly hurt, or worse.

Please.

It was raining, the sort of rain that looked deceptively light but seeped into every fibre and weighed you down; Georgie was glad of the waterproof coat she'd bought the previous month, and even more glad of the drawstring hood.

'We'll start this way,' Ryan said, gesturing diagonally to the hills, 'and we take it in turns calling and listening. We'll walk for fifteen minutes, then turn ninety degrees and walk that way.'

Half an hour of trudging, and she was freezing but she wasn't going to admit it. Worse than the physical discomfort was the coldness and fear inside. She knew that Ryan loved his dog more than anything. If anything had happened to Truffle...

Ryan had never known fear like this.

He was used to losing people. His mum, her family, a string of foster parents. But losing the dog he'd loved since he'd first met her, the only one in his life who hadn't deserted him... The more he thought about it, the worse it was. It wasn't blood pumping through his veins, it was adrenaline; and it wasn't air in his lungs, it was pure solid fear. All that was left was a shallow space that kept him functioning. Just.

Gone.

His dog couldn't be gone.

Truffle was all the family he had.

Was this how the parents of his patients felt, when they sat at their very sick child's bedside? As if the whole world was being sucked into a black hole, every speck of light diminishing?

It was unbearable.

Just putting one foot in front of the other was such an effort that he didn't have the energy to run. Every time he called for his dog, his throat hurt. Every time he listened for an answering bark, his ears felt as if they were buzzing. And every time he glanced at his watch to see if it was time to change direction, he found that only seconds had passed.

How could time move so slowly?

How could this hurt so much?

What if they didn't find her?

Ryan didn't even speak to Georgie. Not that she blamed him. What she'd done was the worst thing ever: she'd lost his dog.

Clara would never have made such a stupid mistake.

If anything had happened to Truffle, Georgie knew she couldn't stay at Hayloft Cottage. She wasn't even sure that she could still work in the same department as Ryan. He'd never, ever, ever forgive her.

The friendship they'd been developing, the attraction they'd both been struggling to ignore—that would turn to sheer hatred in a nanosecond.

Please let them find the dog.

Another ninety-degree turn, more calling, more listening, and still nothing.

They trudged on.

And on.

And then finally she heard a bark. Or was it the wind and she just thought it was a bark because she so desperately wanted to hear the dog?

'I think I just heard something. Call again!' she whispered urgently.

Ryan did so.

It was faint, but this time there was a definite answering bark.

Oh, thank God.

Truffle wasn't dead. Though she might be hurt. They were walking in the direction from where they'd heard Truffle bark, but it didn't sound as if the dog was coming to meet them. When Georgie scanned the area in front of them, she couldn't see any glint from Truffle's reflective collar—a glint that should be there, even in this low light.

She grabbed the torch from her bag and switched it on. Although it was small, the beam was really powerful as it swept the ground in front of them, and finally she caught a glimpse of something reflective. 'Look. I think that's Truffle's collar.'

Except it wasn't moving.

If Truffle had heard them, why wasn't she coming towards them?

Ryan was moving faster than she was, but she didn't try to run after him; the last thing he needed was for her to sprain her ankle or something and need his help getting back to the cottage. She made her way carefully behind him, and when she finally reached him he was on his knees next to the dog, and Truffle was covering his face with licks and making little whimpery noises.

'She's stuck in a rabbit hole,' he said, and she realised that he was digging the dog out with his bare hands. 'Daft beastie. You're not going to disappear into the hills again like that in a hurry, are you?'

The dog wuffed gently and gave a feeble wag of her tail.

'I'm so glad she's all right.' She dropped to her haunches and stroked the Labrador. 'You've been out here for ages, poor girl. I'm so sorry. It was all my fault. You're cold and you're wet, but you must be thirsty.' She took the flask from her bag, removed the lid, and tipped cold water from the bottle into it so the dog could lap at it.

Truffle drank two whole cupsful.

But when Ryan had finished digging her out, it was clear that Truffle wasn't going to be able to walk back to the cottage with them because she was limping badly on the leg that had been trapped in the rabbit hole.

'I don't know if it's a fracture or a sprain,' he said. 'But I'm not risking it getting any worse.' He bent down and lifted her up.

Nearly thirty kilos of wriggly Labrador, but he'd lifted her as if she were a feather.

And his eyes were wet.

Georgie hated herself. Hated that she'd been as careless and thoughtless as Charlie had been towards her.

'Can I do anything to help?' she asked.

'I think you've done enough.'

'Ryan, everyone makes mistakes.'

'Yeah.' A muscle twitched in his jaw. 'This dog is my *family,* and you put her at risk.'

The pain in his voice stopped her biting back any more. 'Do you want me to call the vet?'

'You won't have a signal out here.'

She looked at her phone anyway. But it was a vain hope: of course he was right. He was the local, and she was a stupid, dizzy city girl.

When they finally got back to the cottage, she sat next to Truffle, stroking the top of the dog's head and comforting her while Ryan phoned the vet.

'They're staying open for me so they can take her in,' he said. 'I don't know when I'll be back. Don't wait up.'

She took a deep breath. 'Truffle's clearly in pain and scared, and I'm sure she'd rather have someone sitting with her in the car. So I'll drive you while you're next to her. Don't argue. It's the very least I can do.'

* * *

The very least?

If she'd been more careful in the first place, Truffle wouldn't be hurt now.

Part of Ryan wanted to snarl at Georgie, to tell her to go back to London and leave him the hell alone, but the more sensible part of him knew that she was right.

'All right,' he said, and gave Georgie his car keys, though he couldn't quite bring himself to thank her. 'We'll take my car. It's bigger and she'll be more comfortable with more room.'

'OK. Is the vet's address in your satnav, or do you want to direct me?' she asked.

'I'll direct you.' He carried the dog out to his car and laid her gently on the back seat while Georgie locked the cottage, then told her where to turn to get to the vet's in the next village.

'Well, young Truffle, haven't you been in the wars?' the receptionist said when Ryan carried the dog into the surgery. 'Linda told me you were coming in, Ryan. Go straight through. She's expecting you.'

'Thanks, Carol.'

Linda smiled at him when he entered the exam room. 'Hello, Ryan. Do you want to bring her over here to the table?'

'Thanks.' Gently, he laid the dog down. 'Stay

here, sweetheart. Linda's going to take a look at you.'

Linda checked Truffle's range of movement on all her legs, soothing the dog and talking to her in a low voice as she did so.

'I can feel movement on this leg that really shouldn't be here,' she said. 'I'll do a scan to check that it's definitely a soft tissue problem and not a fracture, but I'm pretty sure It's a grade two sprain. That means she's going to need surgery to stabilise the joint properly. How did she do it?'

'She tunnelled out of the garden, took herself off in the hills, and got stuck in a rabbit hole,' he said. 'I dug her out.'

'Don't be too hard on yourself,' Linda said.

Not so much himself as on Georgie, but anger was still warring with guilt, so he said nothing.

'I've known dogs who've sprained a leg by jumping off a sofa, so it's easily done,' Linda said. 'When did she last eat?'

'This morning.'

'That's good. Do you want to carry her over to the scanner?'

He was glad to have something to do. Waiting really didn't sit well with him. 'Sure.'

He stayed with Truffle, soothing her, while Linda did the scan.

'Good news,' Linda said when she'd finished. 'It's not a fracture, but I do need to stabilise the joint so I'll operate now. She's going to be fine. Though don't look up the operation or anything on the internet,' she added with a smile, 'because you'll panic yourself—just as I'm sure you tell your patients' parents not to look things up while they're waiting.'

He did. And now he knew how it felt from their perspective. Utterly, utterly horrible.

It looked as if there was nothing he could do other than go into the waiting room and—well, *wait*. His eyes prickled and his throat felt full of sand as he stroked Truffle's head and saw her deep brown eyes looking anxious. Oh, dear God, this was unbearable. He looked at Linda. 'Can I stay with her while you give her the anaesthetic? I don't want to leave her—I don't want her to worry about what's going to happen.' Most of all he didn't want the dog to think he'd abandoned her, the way her first owners had.

Linda, who knew Truffle's background, nodded. 'But then I want you out of here so I can concentrate on doing the surgery and not be worrying about you, OK?'

'OK.' He nodded. 'I love you,' he whispered to the dog.

When had he last said those words to a human?

When had someone last said those words to him?

He hated every second that he stood there by the examination table, trying to keep his voice calm as he soothed his dog, stroking her head and then seeing her eyes grow dark as the anaesthetic took over.

If she didn't make it through this he'd never, ever forgive himself.

'She'll be OK,' Linda said again. 'It's a routine operation and I do this all the time.'

Just the sort of thing he said to his patients' parents.

'Go and tell Carol I said to make you a mug of tea with two sugars,' she said with a smile.

'Thanks.' But he felt too sick to drink anything.

Georgie was sitting in the waiting room, her face white and her expression forlorn. 'How is—?' She stopped and covered her hand with her mouth when she realised he was alone. 'Where is she?' she whispered.

'In the operating theatre. It's not a fracture, it's a sprain. Grade two. Linda—the vet—needs to operate to stabilise the joint,' he said.

'I'm so sorry.'

Despite his misery, Ryan knew it wasn't fair

to take out his fear on her. 'Linda said she's seen a dog sprain a leg like that just getting off a sofa. It happens.' He sat down heavily next to her. 'I just have to wait.'

'I'll stay with you,' she said.

Yeah. As if anyone stayed with him for long. 'You don't have to.'

'I want to. There's nothing worse than waiting on your own.'

To his shock, she took his hand. His skin tingled where it touched hers; and it left him feeling even more mixed up. He didn't have a clue what to do now, so he just left his hand where it was, with her fingers curled round his.

She didn't say anything; she was giving him space, he realised. And supporting him at the same time, by just holding his hand. Being there.

And eventually the words started to spill out. He couldn't look at her, but he could talk. Just.

'I'm sorry for snapping at you.'

'It's OK.'

'No, it isn't. But Truffle…' How did he explain? 'She's not just my dog. She's my family.'

'I know.'

She didn't seem to be judging him. 'My *only* family,' he clarified.

Again, she didn't say anything. Didn't ask,

didn't probe, just gave him the space to think and talk when he was ready. Although Georgie hadn't promised to keep everything confidential, he was pretty sure that she would: just as he hadn't said anything to anyone else in the department about her being a widow. She understood how excruciating it was to be gossiped about.

'My mum had me when she was very young,' he said. 'She was sixteen. I don't know who my dad was. She didn't put his name on my birth certificate. And she wouldn't tell anyone who he was, so her parents kicked her out before I was born.'

Georgie said nothing, but her fingers tightened around his. And suddenly it was easy to talk. Easy, for the first time ever.

'She got a flat and a job, and we were doing OK together. But then Mum was killed in an accident when I was six. Someone knocked her off her bike when she was on her way from work to pick me up from school and she wasn't wearing a helmet. She hit her head in the wrong place, and that was it.' He shrugged. 'So that left just me. And her parents—well, they hadn't wanted to know me when she was alive and they told the social worker they didn't want to be lumbered with me. So I went into care.'

* * *

Ryan had been abandoned by his family after his mother had died at the cruelly young age of twenty-two?

Just like his dog had been abandoned by her first owners.

Now Georgie understood just how deeply Ryan identified with his Labrador. No wonder he considered the dog his only family. They were two of a kind.

There were no words. So she just kept holding his hand and giving him the space to talk. He wasn't looking at her; she didn't think his gaze was focused on anything, because his expression was so far away.

'I was an angry six-year-old. I missed my mum and I didn't understand why the hospital couldn't make her better, why she'd died. I couldn't settle anywhere. I wet the bed. I kicked doors and walls. I threw things. I stole. I smashed things up.'

A small, frightened child's equivalent of Truffle and her anxious chewing, Georgie thought.

'So the foster parents didn't tend to keep me for very long. I went through a few sets and then I ended up in a children's home.'

'Your grandparents never changed their minds?'

'No.'

She still couldn't get her head round this. 'And your mum was their only child?'

'Aye.'

How sad. Georgie couldn't understand why any parent would throw their only child onto the street like that. Her parents had been there for Joshua after his wife had died and they'd even offered to come back to London to help, despite the fact they loved their retirement in Norfolk. Just as they'd been there for her after Charlie had been killed, given her a space to stay and to grieve.

If Georgie had fallen pregnant at sixteen, maybe her parents would've been disappointed that her options were narrower than they wanted for her, but they would've supported any decision she made. And they would've helped out with childcare, so she could go on to study and have the career she'd always wanted as well as a baby. And if anything had happened to her, she knew without a doubt that they would've stepped straight in to give her child a home and make sure the child felt loved and wanted. Her elder brother Joshua would've helped, too.

Ryan hadn't had any of that support. He'd made it to where he was completely on his own.

Since his divorce and Clara doing the job swap, all he had was his dog.

'I'm not pitying you,' she said. 'But right now I'm pretty angry on your behalf. And your mum's.'

'There's no need. The McGregors don't deserve any emotion from you,' he said. 'They'll face a lonely old age, instead of having their daughter and their grandson to look in on them and brighten their day with a visit. They were very keen to tell my mother that "as ye sow, so shall ye reap"—the letter they wrote her was in the box of stuff that social services kept for me for when I was old enough. And now they'll perhaps learn the truth of that themselves. I've thought about facing them, but I decided they're not worth it. The best revenge is living well.'

'That's true,' she said. 'And, just so you know, everything you've just told me is going nowhere.'

He looked at her then. 'Thank you.'

'Does Clara know?'

'Yes. She was the one who suggested I get a dog in the first place, when I split up with Zoe.' He gave her a wry smile. 'She said much the same as you. She also said I should try to find my father. So did Zoe. But, as my mother refused to name him, there isn't anyone left to ask.'

'Maybe your mum's best friend from school?' she suggested.

'That's what they suggested,' he said. 'But I don't know who she was. And, even supposing I found someone who was at school with her, someone who remembered her and might help trace her best friend, what if Mum never told anyone at all? And if she did...' He shook his head. 'If my father didn't want to know when she was pregnant or when I was born, he certainly won't want to know thirty-six years later. And I don't want another person in my life who'd let me down.'

So he expected nothing from relationships. Nothing at all.

It was a warning.

And, at the same time, it made her want to weep for the sad, lonely, abandoned little boy he'd been. The lonely, abandoned man he was right now.

It didn't have to stay that way.

But he gently disentangled his fingers from hers, as if to make the point that he was absolutely fine on his own and he'd prefer to keep it that way.

Well, she'd wait with him anyway.

Carol on the reception desk insisted on making them both a mug of tea. And then finally Linda reappeared. 'Do you want the good news, or the good news?' she asked with a smile.

'She's going to be all right?' Ryan asked, sitting up straight.

Linda nodded. 'I've fixed the sprain. She's got a splint and she'll need painkillers, and a strict regime of rest. Walks only on a short leash, and that includes going out to the loo. No running, no jumping, no rough-house playing. And when she's not with you she'll need a cone on.'

'She's going to be bored out of her mind,' Ryan said.

'Get some different puzzle boxes,' Linda said. 'And do lots of mental training with her—stay, nose-touch, and low-activity "find it" games, that sort of thing. And give her toys stuffed with food so she has to work for it—it'll help to keep her occupied.'

'Got it,' Ryan said. 'What's the other good news?'

'She's come round from her op. She's a little bit woozy and a little bit sorry for herself, but you can take her home.'

'Thank you.' Ryan actually hugged Linda, to Georgie's surprise. 'Thank you for making my dog better.'

'Bring her back to see me in a week. Or before that if you think she's got an infection and she's running a temperature, or you're worried about anything at all,' Linda said.

Georgie waited for Ryan to go and collect the dog, and Ryan's eyelashes were suspiciously damp when he carried Truffle back into the waiting room.

'Let's go home,' she said softly.

Then she realised what she'd said. *Home.* Since when had she thought of Hayloft Cottage as home? But she realised it was true. Despite growing up in London and studying and working there ever since, she'd started to think of the wilds of Scotland as home.

CHAPTER SEVEN

RYAN SAT IN the back of his car with Truffle, who seemed woozy and exhausted. There was a patch of shaven skin on her paw where she'd been anaesthetised, her leg had a dressing on it and Ryan had a plastic cone to attach to her collar when he wasn't supervising her, to stop her being able to chew the dressing or nibble at her stitches.

Georgie didn't push him to make conversation; she had a feeling that he was already regretting spilling his heart out to her. Now she knew why his dog was so important to him, it made her feel even worse.

Back at the cottage, she opened doors for him while he carried the dog inside. He set Truffle down on her bed, and the dog's head flopped down between her paws. For a moment, before he masked it, Ryan's face was full of anguish.

And there was nothing she could do, nothing she could say, to make things better.

She fell back on practicalities. 'I'll cook dinner. I bought salmon yesterday.'

'I'm not hungry,' he said.

'Tough. You're eating. You're not going to be any good to Truffle if you keel over. You need food.'

She took his silence as consent and chopped vegetables ready to stir-fry them; she also pan-fried the salmon and put a packet of rice into the microwave.

Ryan looked reluctant to leave the dog when Georgie put their plates on the table.

'She'll be fine. Sit down and eat,' she said.

He made a noncommittal noise but at least he joined her, though he pushed the food around his plate. He ate about half the salmon and rice, and let the rest cool on his plate before going to sit on the floor next to Truffle, hand-feeding the dog some flakes of fish and rice.

Georgie wanted to hug him and tell him everything would be all right, but she thought he'd probably push her away. So she busied herself doing the washing up and pottered round in the kitchen, while the silence stretched out further and further between them.

Eventually she put the kettle on, made them both a mug of tea, and collected his empty plate.

'Sorry,' he muttered. 'And thanks.'

'No problem. Is there anything else I can get you?'

'No.' He took a deep breath. 'I'm going to stay downstairs with her tonight in case she has a delayed reaction to the anaesthetic.'

Oh, no. Georgie hadn't even thought of that, and the idea made her feel sick. Of course they weren't out of the woods yet. The operation was just the first stage. 'Then I'll stay with you to keep you company.'

'There's no need,' Ryan said. 'You've got work tomorrow. I swapped my shift so I've got a day off.'

'I'm still staying with you,' she said. 'Apart from the fact it's my fault Truffle escaped into the hills, two bodies are better than one when it comes to looking after someone who's sick. So I'm going to change into my pyjamas and bring my pillow and duvet down here. And I'll sit with her while you do the same.'

Eventually, he nodded. 'All right. Thanks.'

Once she was downstairs, he went up to change and collect his bedding, and meanwhile Georgie sat talking to Truffle, resting her hand lightly on the dog's side for comfort. 'You're going to be all right, girl,' she promised softly.

When Ryan came downstairs, he put his duvet and pillow on the other side of Truffle.

It reminded Georgie of sleepovers as a child, when a whole bunch of them would sleep in a room and chatter until the small hours. Though Ryan didn't talk. He just lay there, looking worried, and Georgie didn't want to babble platitudes and make things worse for him.

If only she'd double-checked the door.

And, if Truffle developed complications after the operation and the worst happened, Georgie would never forgive herself for taking away the thing that meant most in the world to Ryan.

Eventually, after Ryan had fitted the cone to Truffle's collar, Georgie fell asleep; the next morning, the alarm on her watch woke her, and for a moment she was disorientated. She wasn't in bed: she was lying on the floor. And somehow, during the night, Truffle had moved. The gap between Georgie and Ryan was no longer there: instead, they were lying wrapped in each other's arms.

She kept her eyes tightly shut.

What did she do now?

She hadn't woken in someone's arms since Charlie's death. She was willing to bet it was the same for Ryan, since his divorce.

This closeness had happened while they were asleep. Neither of them had planned this.

Like that kiss in the garden, under the Northern Lights.

If she wriggled out of his arms, the movement would wake him and she'd have to face the embarrassment and awkwardness. If she stayed where she was, she'd have to pretend to be asleep after he woke; given that her breathing was shallow, he'd know that she was awake. And that would lead to awkwardness, too.

There was no easy way out of this.

And then Ryan stirred, and gently disentangled himself from her arms.

OK. He was awake and he'd decided to move first. She'd take her lead from him. She opened her eyes, though she didn't quite dare look him in the eye. 'Morning.'

'Morning,' he said.

But he didn't comment about the way they'd woken up. That was good. He clearly wanted to avoid the awkwardness, too. 'How's Truffle?' she asked.

The dog's tail thumped on the floor as she responded to her name.

'She looks OK,' Ryan said, and took the cone off. 'Want to go out, girl? I'm afraid it'll have to be on the lead. I can't risk you rushing about and knocking your leg.'

Georgie sneaked a tiny glance while he took Truffle to the kitchen door and pulled on his boots and a coat over his pyjamas. Dishevelled from sleep, he was utterly gorgeous. And it made all her senses hum with longing. But right now they still had fences to mend between them so she needed to put a lid on that reaction.

She got to her feet. Keeping busy was the way she usually dealt with things.

By the time he came back in with the dog, she'd made coffee and laid the table for breakfast.

'You didn't have to do that.'

'I wanted breakfast, and it's as quick to make it for two as for one,' she said.

He looked exhausted. The worry and the emotions from yesterday had clearly taken it out of him.

'Thanks.'

She didn't push him to talk, but after breakfast when he went to have a shower she finished the washing up, then sat on the floor with the dog.

'I'm so sorry about what happened,' she said, stroking the top of Truffle's head. 'It was totally my fault and I shouldn't have been careless with you. I know what it feels like when someone's careless with you.' She bit her lip. 'I feel bad that I hurt Ryan as much as Charlie hurt me. I don't know how I'm going to make it up to him, but I'm just going to have to try harder.'

* * *

I hurt Ryan as much as Charlie hurt me.

The words echoed in Ryan's head and he couldn't quite make sense of them.

From what Georgie had told him, Charlie had been a hero. He'd been killed in a landslide while he'd been out helping in an earthquake disaster zone. And she'd been crying a few days ago on her wedding anniversary, which told Ryan that she was still deeply in mourning for her late husband.

But now he wondered. How deeply would you mourn someone who'd hurt you?

She'd said that someone had been careless with her, and that Charlie had hurt her. Were those two statements related or separate? What had happened?

Not that he could ask. He'd have to wait until Georgie was ready to talk about it—if she ever was. But, with this and the couple of things she'd already let slip, it seemed everything hadn't been quite as wonderful in her marriage as he'd originally thought.

He walked more heavily down the stairs so she'd be aware of his presence; it would give her time to get herself together if she needed to.

'Thank you for keeping an eye on Truffle for me,' he said when he went into the living room.

'It's the least I could do.' She paused. 'I've

been thinking—maybe we should look at the roster again and try to move our shifts so one of us is on an early while the other's on a late, so Truffle has company as much as possible. And if you can teach me what sort of things to do to keep her occupied, I'll do my best.'

She really was trying hard to make up for what she'd done.

And, now he was pretty sure Truffle was going to be all right, his anger had dissipated. 'Thank you. And I'm sorry I took it out on you yesterday, when I was worried about Truffle. It wasn't fair of me.'

She lifted her chin. 'I deserved everything you said. You'd warned me she's an absconder. I should have checked the door properly. The stupid thing is, in London I would've double-checked; I know it's no excuse, but here it feels safer.'

'Here, it *is* safer,' he said.

'But I still should've checked, and I'm sorry. And I was going to say to you yesterday, I'll cover the vet's bill because it was my fault.'

'She's insured,' he said. 'But I appreciate the back-up for keeping her occupied. She's going to be bored.'

'Just tell me what the doggy equivalent to reading a gazillion stories and doing art stuff is,' she said.

'Is that what you do with your niece?'

'That and dancing,' she said. 'But you want Truffle to rest physically as much as possible, right? So not the doggy equivalent of dancing.'

He could imagine Georgie sitting with her niece on her lap, reading stories, or at the table, drawing and making models from play dough. And from there it was a tiny step to imagining her doing that with her own child. A little girl who was the spit of her mother—but with grey eyes and dark auburn hair, like his own.

Oh, help.

He'd never imagined himself as a father before. Not with Zoe, even though he'd loved her. But maybe that was because he and Zoe hadn't been quite the right fit.

Was he the right fit with Georgie?

The idea sent him into a flat spin. He was worried sick about the one constant in his life, the dog he regarded as his entire family. Right now, he didn't have the headspace to face the ghosts of his past and work out whether he could deal with them.

Knowing that he was being a coward, but doing it anyway, he said, 'I'll just go and get some more bread from the farm shop before you leave for work, if that's OK?'

'Sure. Truffle and I are going to watch a rerun of *Friends*,' she said.

She was actually sitting on the floor with the dog now, taking as much care of her as Ryan would himself, and it made him feel as if something had cracked around his heart. Something that started to let the light in.

The feeling intensified over the next couple of days. Georgie was really, really good with Truffle. She was patient, she kept the dog amused and helped tire her out so she wasn't fractious. He could trust her with his dog; so maybe, even though the idea of letting anyone that close to him terrified him, he could trust her with himself. Trust that even when her six-month job swap was up, she'd work with him to find a way for them to stay together.

But she was behaving more like a best friend than anything else. How could he explain to her that his feelings towards her were changing—that he was starting to want things he'd always believed he didn't? And that he wanted them with her?

Sharing a house with Ryan was driving Georgie crackers. He'd made it very clear that he wanted nothing more than friendship from her—that he didn't want to get involved with anyone again, and he wasn't going to act on the attraction between them, despite that kiss.

Maybe a mad fling would get him out of her system.

But Georgie didn't want a mad fling. If anything was going to happen between them, she wanted more than one night; she wanted to see where it would take them.

Which left them at stalemate, because Ryan McGregor was one of the most stubborn men she'd ever met.

She was working in the PAU at lunchtime on the Saturday when a four-year-old girl came in. Jennie had had a cold, which had then turned into a cough that wouldn't go away. Her mum said it was worse at night but thought all colds were like that; and now Jennie was struggling to breathe, her chest was wheezy and she'd complained of chest pain. There was obvious sucking in at the base of her throat.

All the signs told Georgie that this was probably asthma, but she wanted to run an ECG to check the little girl's heart. She went in search of someone to help her do the ECG while she did a full examination, and Ryan just happened to be in the corridor.

'Everything OK?' he asked.

'No, I have a patient with suspected asthma and I want to run an ECG, so I need someone in with me to do that while I help her with her breathing.'

'I'll do it,' he said.

He was too senior for this, really, but she wasn't going to argue; she wanted to help her patient *now*.

She took him back to the treatment room and introduced him to Jennie and her mum.

'Is there any asthma or hay fever or allergies in your family?' Ryan asked.

Jennie's mum shook her head. 'Not in her dad's, either. Is that what you think it is?'

'It's possible,' Georgie said. 'But we'll concentrate on getting Jennie breathing easily before we run some tests.'

'Can you sit up straight for us, Jennie?' Ryan asked. 'That'll make it easier for you to breathe.'

The little girl nodded, a tear running down her face, and sat up straight.

'That's really good,' Georgie said. 'Now I'd like you to breathe in through your nose and out through your mouth. Take it slowly. All the way in, all the way out.'

She guided Jennie through the breathing; once the little girl seemed calmer, she fitted a blue inhaler into a spacer. 'This is special medication to help you breathe,' she said. 'I want you to hold the tube for me, and put the mouthpiece in your mouth. I'm going to press this bit on the end to put the medicine in the tube and I want you to breathe in to make the tube whistle for me. Can you do that?'

Jennie nodded again, and did what Georgie asked.

'That's brilliant,' Ryan said. 'You're being so brave.' He glanced at his watch and counted off a minute. 'Another big breath in of the medicine?'

They repeated a puff of the inhaler per minute for ten puffs, then checked Jennie's oxygen saturation levels. Ryan distracted Jennie with a series of terrible jokes while Georgie took bloods, and then Georgie put sticky pads on Jennie's chest so they could run an ECG.

'The pattern on this paper is a picture of how your heart is beating,' Ryan said. 'And that's beautifully normal.'

Jennie's mum looked relieved. 'So is it asthma?' she asked.

'Coughing and wheezing can be caused by things other than asthma,' Georgie said, 'and Jennie's too young to do some of the tests to show how her lungs are working, so I know this is going to be frustrating but we'll need to do a trial of treatment for the next few weeks.'

'We can give you a blue inhaler and a spacer like this one for her to use when she has bad symptoms,' Ryan said. 'The inhaler will give Jennie a dose of corticosteroids—they're the ones the body produces naturally, not the ones you hear of bodybuilders taking—and using it in the form of an inhaler means that the medicine goes straight into her airways. It'll open them up and help keep her safe while we're trying to work out what's causing the problem.'

'And we'll need you to keep a diary for your doctor,' Georgie said. 'So when Jennie has symptoms, write down what they are, the date and time, what the weather's like and what's happening at the time—so if there's a pet nearby, or it's really cold, or she was running about. I can print something out for you to make it easier to remember.'

'Thank you,' Jennie's mum said.

'This is going to sound a bit callous,' Ryan said, 'but when she's wheezing or coughing, if you record her on your phone it will really help your doctor or the asthma nurse hear what her symptoms are like.'

'And then if you can write down how many puffs she takes of the inhaler, and whether that helps her, it stays the same or it gets worse,' Georgie said. 'The more information you can give, the more it will help your doctor to spot the patterns and make a firm diagnosis.'

'I'll make sure I do that,' Jennie's mum said.

'That's great,' Georgie said. 'I'll give you an action plan for the next couple of months so you can share it with Jennie's nursery, your family and friends, so then they'll know what to do if she gets any asthma symptoms. The action plan tells you how to spot the early signs of problems and what to do.'

'If she needs to use an inhaler more than three times a week,' Ryan said, 'then your asthma nurse will give you a brown preventer inhaler, which Jennie needs to take every day to help stop her getting the symptoms in the first place. But let's see how we go in the next couple of months. Obviously, if you're worried, see your doctor; and if the inhaler doesn't help, bring her straight back here.'

'Thank you,' Jennie's mum said.

Ryan crouched down so he was at Jennie's level. 'You've been really brave.' He produced a sparkly 'I was brave' sticker from his pocket. 'So I think you deserve this.'

'Thank you,' Jennie said shyly.

Georgie printed out the action plan and asthma diary for Jennie's mum, and helped her fill it in. 'We'll obviously send all the details to your family doctor, but do go and make an appointment to see the asthma specialist in eight weeks' time.'

'I will,' Jennie's mum promised, and took her daughter's hand.

Why was it, Georgie wondered, that she and

Ryan were so in tune at work, virtually able to finish each other's sentences—and yet when it came to their personal life, he backed away from her? She really thought they could be good together.

But if Ryan wasn't prepared to give them a chance, there was nothing she could do to change his mind. She'd have to give up. And next year, when she went back to London, he'd fade out of her life.

CHAPTER EIGHT

'ONLY A MEAL for one tonight?' Janie asked, looking surprised.

'It's the departmental night out,' Ryan explained. 'I'm staying at home with Truffle so Georgie can go.'

'If Truffle hadn't had her accident, would you have been going?' Janie asked.

Ryan grimaced. 'Probably. Though only because I wouldn't have had a good excuse *not* to go.'

'What's the problem?' Janie asked.

'It's a ceilidh.' If he didn't dance with Georgie, people would notice and start speculating; if he did dance with her, he'd end up thinking of the night he'd kissed her and the morning she'd woken in his arms. Which would be a bad idea for both of them, because he still hadn't sorted his head out.

'Dancing's good for you. You're a doctor, so

you should know that,' Janie said with a grin. 'What's the real problem?'

His head was completely mixed up when it came to Georgie: though he wasn't telling Janie *that*. 'I delegated the organisation to one of my colleagues. She says all the men have to wear kilts.'

'And you don't have one?' She smiled at him. 'No problem. My Donald's about your size. He can lend you one.'

'I have a kilt,' Ryan said.

'Then there's no problem, is there?' Janie said. 'Truffle can have a sleepover with me and Donald, so you don't have to worry about getting back early for her. You work hard enough. You deserve a break. A night out will do you good.' She took the foil tray of casserole from his basket. 'I'm not selling you that. You go dancing in that kilt. And no arguments from you, or I'll text Clara and she'll nag you.'

Ryan knew when to give in. So he duly dropped Truffle at Janie's, showered and changed into his kilt.

When he came downstairs, Georgie was ready. 'I'll drive us, if you like.'

For a moment, he couldn't answer because his tongue felt stuck to the roof of his mouth. Georgie looked amazing. Her hair was up, and she was wearing just enough mascara to make her green eyes look huge, and red lipstick that made her mouth look temptingly kissable. She was wearing heels, making her legs look as if they went on for ever; though her sleeveless red dress was very demure, with a skirt that came down to just below her knee and a rounded neckline that just skimmed her collarbones. And he was filled with the urge to take her into his arms and do one of those complicated dance moves that would spin her out and let her skirt swish round, then spin her back so she was in his arms again.

'Ryan? Is everything all right?'

He gathered himself together. 'It's fine. No, I'll drive and you can have a glass of wine or whatever,' he said.

'All right.' She coughed. 'You look very nice.'

He took a deep breath and hoped that his voice sounded normal when he said, 'As do you.' He gestured to the door. 'Let's go.'

'Very nice' didn't even begin to describe how Ryan McGregor looked in a kilt.

Georgie had only ever seen men wearing kilts on TV or in the movies. She wasn't prepared for just how good the outfit looked in real life. She had no idea what the black and grey tartan was—she planned to look it up surreptitiously online, rather than embarrass herself by asking him—but it suited him, particularly as it was teamed with a Prince Charlie jacket with ornate buttons, a waistcoat, a sporran, a wing-collar shirt and a black bow tie. His shoes were highly polished, his socks showed off very well-formed knees, and she went hot all over when she remembered all the suggestions about exactly what a Scot wore under his kilt.

Oh, help.

The last thing he needed was her behaving like a schoolgirl with a huge crush.

Even though she *did* have a huge crush on him.

More than a crush. She was more than half-way to falling in love with this dour, difficult man—a man who had a huge heart and had so much to give, but kept himself closed off.

He didn't say much on the way into the city, and she walked beside him to the club where they were meeting the rest of the team, not having a clue where they were going.

Parminder and the others were waiting outside; and, as Parm had decreed, every single one of the men was wearing a kilt. Some were wearing a casual ghillie shirt, and others had chosen the more formal option of wing collar and Prince Charlie jacket, but not a single one could hold a candle to Ryan in the gorgeousness stakes.

'I have to say I'm very impressed,' she said with a smile. 'Excellent organisation on your part, Parm, and what a handsome team we have. You all scrub up rather nicely.'

Alistair grinned at her and did a pirouette. 'Some of us more so than others.'

'You look very pretty in your skirt, Al,' she teased.

'*Skirt*,' he huffed, laughing. 'I'll have you know that's my clan tartan and an eight-yard kilt you're talking about.' He gave her a lascivious wink. 'If you're very good, I'll tell you what I keep in my sporran.'

'Yeah, yeah,' she retorted, laughing back because she knew Alistair was completely harmless and just teasing her.

'Now we're all here, let's go in,' Parminder said. 'The first half of the night's a proper ceilidh, and then it's general dancing.'

The hall was wonderful; the overhead lights were turned down low and fairy lights draped the walls and the columns, making the place seem magical. A band was playing on a stage at one end, and there was a caller to organise everything.

Their team joined the dance floor for the next set of reels, and Georgie enjoyed herself hugely.

Then, while the band had a break, the caller acted as a DJ and streamed music through the sound system.

Alistair turned out to be as terrible a dancer as he'd told her he was, but Georgie and Parminder helped him as much as they could. And at least dancing with Alistair stopped her making a fool of herself by falling at Ryan's feet, she thought. She danced with all the men from their ward; she danced with what felt like everyone in the whole room for the next few sets of reels; and the only person she hadn't danced with properly was Ryan.

Was he avoiding her?

But then the band left the stage and the caller went back to playing recorded music, this time slowing things down. Couples took to the floor, dancing cheek to cheek, and loneliness flowed over Georgie like a wave.

She'd loved dancing with Charlie.

But Charlie wasn't here any more. Even if he hadn't been killed by the landslide, he probably wouldn't have been with her. He would've been with his new family—the family he hadn't wanted to have with her.

She was lost in thought when Ryan walked over to her.

'May I?'

Her head was suddenly too jumbled to find words, so she nodded.

He drew her into his arms and held her close, dancing cheek to cheek with her. Just as they'd been that night under the stars, watching the Northern Lights. Georgie thought of the way he'd kissed her then and it felt as if all the air had hissed out of her lungs.

This was just a dance. Just a dance. If she told herself that often enough, she'd believe it.

Yet he seemed to be drawing her closer still, and her arms were tightly wrapped round him.

Everything around them vanished; all she was aware of was Ryan, the warmth and tautness of his body and his clean masculine scent.

She wasn't sure which of them moved first, but then his lips were brushing against hers, light as a butterfly's wing and sensitising every nerve-ending. And she was kissing him back, tiny nibbles that segued into something deeper, more sensual.

When he broke the kiss, his grey eyes were almost black in the low light. 'Let's get out of here.' His voice was husky, almost rusty, with desire.

They were by the door. Nobody would notice them leave; nobody would gossip. Their colleagues would assume they'd gone back early to check on Truffle. 'Yes,' she said.

To her relief, they didn't bump into anyone from the department when they collected their coats. And Ryan didn't chat to her as they headed back to his car; though he held her hand all the way, and every so often he stopped to kiss her beneath a lamp-post. And he held her hand all the way back to the cottage, only breaking contact when he needed to change gear.

By the time they were back at the cottage, Georgie was almost quivering in anticipation.

Maybe this was an insane thing to do. Or maybe this was what both of them needed, to help them move on. Maybe actually giving in to the way they reacted to each other physically would sort both their heads out and they'd find this whole thing wasn't complicated after all.

He shrugged his coat off, then removed hers. 'Dance with me again?' he asked.

She nodded, and he found something slow and sweet on his phone before taking her back in his arms.

This time, when he kissed her, she didn't have to worry about who might see and gossip about it. It was just the two of them in the low light of the single lamp he'd switched on.

This time, when he broke the kiss, his eyes held a challenge. 'So where do we go from here?'

'My room.'

'Are you sure?'

Meaning that if she said no, he'd back off. He wouldn't push her into anything she wasn't ready to do. 'Very sure,' she said. 'I've wanted this since the night you kissed me under the stars.'

He stroked her face. 'I made a wish on a falling star.'

That this would happen? 'Good.' She reached up on tiptoe and kissed him again.

His pupils dilated a fraction further. 'I want to turn caveman and carry you to bed,' he said. 'But a spiral staircase isn't the best idea and I don't want to drop you.'

'I've got a better one,' she said, and kicked off her shoes before taking his hand and leading him up the stairs.

At the doorway to her room, he kissed her again.

'That dress. Since I first saw you in it, I wanted to do one of those flashy dance moves that makes your skirt twirl out, then spin you back into my arms.' His breath caught. 'And I want to take it off you.'

'That kilt and that jacket,' she said. 'It makes you look hot.' She felt her face grow warm. 'And your wild hair.'

'It's wild because I can't be bothered to visit the barber every month.'

She stroked his face. 'It makes you look like a Scottish chieftain.'

'I'll run with that,' he said. 'Which means I get to do this.' He slid his hand up her spine, making her arch her back, then slid the zip down very, very slowly. His gaze was intense as it held hers, and he pushed the material gently off her shoulders; her dress slid to the floor in a puddle. Colour slashed across his cheeks and he drew in a sharp breath. 'Well, now, Dr Jones.' He scooped her up in his arms, clearly with the intention of carrying her to her bed.

'Not so fast,' she said.

'No?' He went very still.

'No. Because you're wearing too much,' she said. 'We need to even that up first.'

Then he smiled. 'What do you suggest, Dr Jones?'

'There are two ways we can do this. The first,' she said, 'is that you set me back on my feet and let me undress you. The second is that you carry me to my bed and then strip for me.'

His smile grew more sensual. 'And your preferred course?'

'I don't know,' she admitted. 'I'm greedy. I kind of want both.'

'Compromise, then.' He set her back on her feet. 'Do the jacket.'

The buttons on his jacket weren't fastened, so it was easy to remove; but the matching buttons on the waistcoat were incredibly ornate and it took her a while to undo them. His bow tie was next—a proper one, she noticed, not a pre-tied one that clipped on. As she undid the buttons of his shirt, his breathing grew quicker and more shallow. She untucked the shirt from the waistband of his kilt, then slid the material over his shoulders, letting it fall to the floor.

Bare-chested, he was beautiful. There was a light sprinkling of hair on his chest, and his abdomen was flat. But there was no vanity in him: he simply looked after himself properly. 'Perfect,' she whispered.

This time, when he scooped her up into his arms, her skin slid against his, and desire flickered low in her belly.

He kissed her again, hard, and laid her down against the pillows.

'So you wanted me to strip for you.'

'Partly because I have no idea how a kilt fastens,' she admitted.

He chuckled. 'Buckles, Dr Jones. Buckles. And a kilt pin, to preserve your modesty when you sit down.'

Was he telling her that he wasn't wearing anything underneath the kilt?

She went hot all over.

'First, the sporran,' he said.

'What exactly is a sporran?' she asked.

'The word's Gaelic for "pocket",' he said, 'and that's exactly what it is. It's where I keep my keys and my wallet. Putting a pocket in a kilt would spoil the line.'

'Uh-huh.'

He undid the buckle at the back before dropping it on the floor with his jacket.

'Then the kilt pin.'

'Give me a twirl,' she said.

He grinned, and did so—meaning she got to see the perfect musculature in his back.

'Then the buckles,' he whispered. 'Except I need to do some tidying first.'

'Tidying?' She couldn't think straight. She was still trying to work out what he was wearing under that kilt.

'Aye. Tidying.' He picked up her dress and hung it neatly over the back of the chair, hanging his jacket, waistcoat and shirt over the top of it.

Now she understood.

Ryan McGregor was a man who took care of things.

Next, he took off his socks. 'Because there's an order to underwear,' he added.

And a man wearing nothing but socks wasn't sexy. 'Excellent idea,' she said.

He held her gaze, then, and undid first the lower buckle on his right hip and then the upper. He held it with his left hand, while he crossed his left hand over to his right hip to undo the final buckle.

'And once the buckles are done,' he said, his voice low and sexy, 'you take the kilt off.' He turned away from her, and removed the kilt…

…to reveal soft black jersey shorts that clung to him.

'So a Scotsman *does* wear something under his kilt, then,' she said, her voice shaky.

'This one does, aye.' He placed the kilt neatly on the other clothes on the back of the chair, and gave her the most scorching look. 'But close your eyes and hold that thought.'

He was going shy on her, after looking at her like *that*?

OK. She'd run with it.

She closed her eyes. But when the bed still didn't dip under his weight, she opened her eyes.

She was alone in the room.

Clearly he'd changed his mind.

She was about to get up and close the door,

when he reappeared. 'You were supposed to keep your eyes closed and hold that thought,' he said. 'Because there's something important I needed.'

Then she saw the little box in his hand. Condoms. Again, he was being careful with her, and she appreciated it.

'Since you opened your eyes,' he said, 'I think it's my turn.'

'Your turn?'

'For the show. You're wearing more than me.'

'Taking off my tights isn't sexy.'

He raised an eyebrow. 'Are you asking me to do it?'

She sucked in a breath. 'Yes.'

'Then your wish is my command,' he said, giving her a deep bow.

He placed the box of condoms on her bedside table, then sat on the bed next to her and slid his fingers underneath the waistband of her tights before gently drawing them downwards. With one hand, he urged her to lift her bottom from the bed so he could take the nylon down further; and then he peeled the tights off achingly slowly, caressing every bit of skin as he uncovered it.

By the time he'd finished, Georgie was quivering.

She wasn't sure which of them removed

which bit of clothing next, because by then everything was blurred by desperate need; all she was aware of was how badly she wanted him and how her temperature felt as if it had risen a thousand degrees.

Ryan kissed her, his mouth sensual and persuading, until she was a quivering mess; but it still wasn't enough to sate her desire. She wanted more. *So much more.*

She must've said it out loud, because at last he moved between her thighs.

'Are you sure about this?' he asked.

'I'm a bit out of practice, but I'm very sure,' she whispered.

He reached over to take a condom from the box.

She curled her fingers round his. 'Let me.'

'Of course,' he said, and his smile was so sexy that she felt the pulse beating hard between her legs.

The past didn't matter any more. All that mattered was this man, here and now, and how much she wanted him.

She undid the foil packet and caressed his hard length, making him gasp with pleasure, then rolled the condom on.

'Now?' he asked.

'Now,' she whispered.

He eased inside her, gaze intense and focused

on hers. It should've been awkward and faintly embarrassing, the first time, but it just felt so *right*.

Then he began to move. 'Keep your eyes open,' he said.

And she did. Instead of closing her eyes and giving up to the sensations shimmering through her, she watched his eyes, his face. She could see her own desire reflected there, the need.

And then she felt her climax splintering through her, felt his body tighten against hers and heard his answering cry.

He held her for a few moments longer, then went to deal with the condom.

When he came back, he went to pick up his discarded clothes.

'Don't go,' she said.

She could see the emotions running through his expression—longing, as if he wanted to stay, and regret, as if he thought it'd be a bad idea to let her this close.

'Just for tonight,' she said. They could deal with the fallout tomorrow. But she wanted tonight first.

As if he guessed what she was thinking, Ryan nodded and slid into bed beside her, drawing her into his arms. Georgie curled against him, feeling warmer and happier than she had for a very long time, and finally fell asleep.

* * *

The next morning, Ryan was the first to wake.

He didn't regret last night—he was so glad he'd had that moment of closeness with her, because it had been everything he'd hoped it would be—but this whole thing made him feel seriously antsy. If he got this wrong, they'd both end up hurt.

He shifted so he could see her as she slept. She was so sweet, so gorgeous and so giving.

Maybe he should get out of the bed without waking her, and then they could face this when they were both fully clothed; but he couldn't bring himself to abandon her.

And then her eyes opened.

'Hello,' she said, all pink-cheeked and shy and adorable.

He desperately wanted to kiss her, but that would complicate things. 'Hello,' he said softly.

His feelings must have shown on his face, because her eyes narrowed slightly. 'You're not OK with this, are you?'

'It's not you. It's me.'

'Uh-huh. That's what men say when they want to make themselves feel less guilty.'

He raked a hand through his hair. 'I'm not trying to make myself feel less guilty. But I shouldn't have even kissed you last night. It wasn't fair to you.'

'Because you're still in love with your ex and you're not ready to move on?'

'No. I'm not still in love with my ex.'

'Then why?'

'Because,' he said, 'I'm not good at relationships and I shouldn't have led you on.'

'Uh-huh.'

He grimaced. 'I need to be honest with you. It's my fault my marriage broke up. I loved Zoe, and she loved me, and I honestly never meant to hurt her.'

'You cheated on her?'

Why on earth had she assumed that? 'No. I would never have done that. But I still hurt her. She wanted me to let her close. She wanted to have children. And I couldn't do either of those things.'

The expression on her face told him she was assuming he meant he was infertile, and she could think of plenty of solutions. He needed to tell her the truth.

'Not that I couldn't—I wouldn't,' he corrected himself. 'Since I was six, I'd learned to rely on myself and not let people close. Zoe couldn't change that. Neither of us wanted children when we got married—we were both focused on our careers. But then things changed. Her biological clock started ticking, and mine didn't.' He shrugged. 'Having children or not having children isn't something you can compromise on. One of you has to lose. But I never pretended to be someone I wasn't.'

'Charlie pretended,' she said, surprising him.

'How?'

'He was seeing someone else,' she said. 'Every time he went somewhere to help after a disaster, she was there as well.'

Ryan stared at her, shocked. Now he knew why she'd leapt to that conclusion earlier: because it had happened to her before. Her husband had cheated on her. 'That's horrible. I'm sorry.'

'He lied to her, too. He told her he wasn't married.'

He knew it was rude and intrusive but he couldn't help asking. 'How did you find out about it?'

'Her parents wrote to me at the hospital. He'd told Trish that I was his sister. They wanted to know if they could come to his funeral, or if I wanted to go to Trish's. They talked about him, said how much Trish had loved him. I hadn't had a clue.' She swallowed hard. 'I think I broke their hearts even further when I called them to explain that Charlie was an only child and I was his wife. And they kind of broke mine a bit more when they told me Trish had been expecting his baby.'

He remembered she'd said something about expecting to be a mum by this point in her life. 'Had you been…?'

She shook her head. 'We'd planned to. But then, when we got to the point where we'd planned to start trying, Charlie changed his mind. He kept coming up with reasons why we should wait a bit. So clearly he didn't want to make a family with me.'

Which had clearly hurt her. He was glad he hadn't kept Zoe hanging on a string like that.

'I don't know whether he even knew she was pregnant. She might not have had a chance to tell him, because they'd only been out there for a couple of days when they were killed, and she might've wanted to wait for the right moment before telling him.' She dragged in a breath. 'She was four months gone. If they'd lived, the baby would've been crawling by now.'

'That's tough,' he said. 'I'm sorry he cheated on you and I'm sorry you found out that way.' He paused. 'How did his parents react?'

'I didn't tell them,' she said. 'I thought about it. But what was the point? Everyone thought Charlie was a hero. And he was. He was a brilliant emergency doctor, and he went out to help in disaster areas.'

'And he cheated on you and lied to his mistress,' Ryan pointed out. In his view, the way Charlie had treated his wife pretty much cancelled his hero status.

'That wasn't relevant to anyone else,' she said. 'His family, his friends—they were all mourning the man they loved, the man they'd respected. What was the point of making them all feel worse? What would it achieve, telling his parents that their only son had been about to give them a much-wanted grandchild but oh, by the way, said grandchild was killed along with his father?'

'How did you live with that, though? Knowing Charlie wasn't the man they all thought he was, and pretending that you agreed with them—when really you weren't just mourning the man you married, you were hurt by his betrayal?'

She spread her hands. 'He wasn't there to defend himself or explain himself. It wouldn't have been fair to tell everyone the truth.'

'It wasn't fair to you, *not* telling the truth,' Ryan pointed out.

'That's really why I wanted to get away from London. Not just because I was sick of the pity, but I was near to cracking and blurting it out, and then the pity would've been so much worse.'

'And you didn't tell anyone at all? Not even your best friend?'

'I didn't know how.' She bit her lip. 'I told my brother. But only because he was so upset that I was bailing out on him, so I thought I owed him the truth. He was so angry on my behalf. But I swore him to secrecy.'

'I think you're a nicer person than I am. I would've told people the truth.'

'What was the point?' Georgie asked again. 'It wouldn't have achieved anything except hurting people who were already hurting. His parents had suffered enough. And they're nice people. They didn't deserve to have their illusions shattered.' She sat up and wrapped her arms round her knees. 'I still wonder what would've happened if Charlie and Trish hadn't been caught in that landslide. Would he have left me for her? Would they have brought up their child together?'

'Don't torture yourself,' Ryan said. 'You'll never know and it didn't happen.'

'No, but I have to face that I wasn't enough to keep Charlie happy. Otherwise he wouldn't have looked elsewhere. There's obviously something wrong with me.'

Ryan was outraged on her behalf. How could she possibly think that she was the one at fault? 'There's nothing wrong with you.'

'No?' But Georgie didn't quite dare voice what was in her head. If there wasn't something lacking in her, then she would've been enough for Charlie and she would be enough for Ryan— and she clearly wasn't enough for him, or he wouldn't be backing away from her right now at the speed of light.

'There's really nothing wrong with you,' he confirmed. 'Nothing at all. Any man would be lucky to have you in his life.'

Did he include himself in that?

She'd ducked the issue last night, because she'd really wanted to be held, to sleep in his arms. She'd wanted to make love with him. She had no regrets at all. But she wasn't a coward. She knew the reckoning came now, and she was going to face it. 'So where does that leave us?'

He looked haunted. 'I like you, Georgie. I like you a lot. I think we could be good together.'

Hope leaped in her heart. Was he going to give them a chance?

'*But*.'

The hope came crashing back down again. Stupid. Of course there was a but.

He took a deep breath. 'This whole thing scares me spitless. You want children. I never thought that was where my life would take me. It's so easy to get things wrong, to make a mistake. We've both been hurt. And taking a risk with you... I'm not sure I can do this.'

She looked at him. 'Can I ask you something?'

He gave her a wary look. 'What?'

'I accept that you don't want children. But can I ask *why*?'

He raked a hand through his hair. 'You know about my background. After my mum died, nobody wanted me. I don't want to put a child through that.'

'Understood,' she said. 'But if your mum hadn't been knocked off her bike, she would've loved you. She might have met someone and you would've gained a ready-made family.'

'But that didn't happen.'

'And,' she said, 'there's another difference. If you had a child—if anything happened to you, that child would still have a mum and a family who loved him or her. Or if anything happened to your partner, your child would still have you.'

'True,' he said. 'But I don't remember what it's like to be a son. I didn't grow up with a male role model. How do I know I'd be any good as a dad?'

'Because,' she said, 'I've seen you at work. You care for your patients as if they're your own flesh and blood. I've seen you sit with a young child in your break and read stories, or just chat to one of the older ones.'

'I'm merely keeping them from being bored, so they don't disrupt the ward,' he said.

She thought there was more to it than that. She'd noticed he spent time with kids who didn't have a family. That wasn't the act of a man who didn't like children. 'And Truffle.' His rescue dog. 'You love her. You make sure she's fed and exercised and feels loved.'

'That's different.'

'It isn't, Ryan. You treat her the way that other men would treat their child. You've told me yourself that she's your family. So don't try to kid yourself. You're putting all these barriers in the way, but they're not as big as you think they are. And you're not going to be on your own if you try to get over them.'

He shook his head. 'I don't want to hurt you, Georgie. But you need to know I'm really not good at relationships.'

Pain lanced through her. He was giving up on them that easily? He didn't think she was worth the effort? 'So you're saying we call it a halt?'

'I think that's the best thing.'

'Because you're too scared to take a chance.'

His eyes widened. 'So you think I'm a coward?'

'No, I don't think you're a coward,' she said. 'I think you're scared and you're stubborn and you've decided that everything's set in a certain way. But life isn't like that, Ryan. It's flexible. Things change. It's not about being perfect and getting things right all the time. It's about trying, about learning to compromise and realising it's OK if something goes a different way from the way you'd planned it.'

Did she have to spell it out for him?

Maybe. It was a risk. But, if she didn't take it, she knew she'd always regret it. 'All you have to do is reach out.' Reach out, and she'd be there.

'All you have to do is reach out.'

Did Georgie have any idea how hard that was?

She'd clearly grown up being dearly loved. To the point where she was careful with other people—even though Charlie had hurt her badly with his affair and the baby, she'd still thought about his family and friends and protected their happy memories rather than tarnish them with the painful truth. Ryan wasn't sure he could've been that noble, in her shoes.

And he didn't think he could reach out and grab what she was offering. Deep down, he didn't think he deserved it. Otherwise someone would've tried to keep him before, wouldn't they? His grandparents, his foster parents—all the people who hadn't wanted him enough. Zoe had given up on him. Why would it be any different with Georgie?

'I can't,' he said.

She looked sad. 'You're not even going to try, are you?'

'No,' he said. He felt guilty and miserable, but he couldn't change who he was. He knew he'd only disappoint Georgie. It was better to back off now and keep his heart intact than to let himself believe that someone could really love him, and then learn the hard way that he'd fooled himself again.

'Thank you for being honest.' She lifted her chin. 'I'll find somewhere else to live for the rest of the job swap.'

'No. I'm the one causing the problem, so I ought to be the one to move out.'

She shook her head. 'As you told me, landlords don't like renting places to someone with a dog, particularly a dog who chews. So it'll be easier for me to be the one to go.'

This was when he was supposed to agree. She was giving him what he'd asked for. He couldn't give her what she wanted, so he should just let her go.

So why did his mouth open and the words, 'Don't go,' come out?

She just stared at him.

Maybe this was the best compromise. 'Don't go,' he said again. 'We can be adult about this. We can ignore the—' Well, he had to admit to that much. 'We can ignore the attraction between us, just as we do at work.'

'Says the man who made love with me last night and even now is sitting in my bed,' she said wryly.

'I'm sorry. I wish I could be different, I really do. But I can't. I've tried in the past and I've never really been able to let anyone close to me. If that's what you want from me, all I'll do is hurt you and I don't want to do that.' He took a deep breath. 'I don't regret last night, and I definitely don't regret being with you. But I am what I am. I'm sorry I can't be who you want me to be.'

'Thank you,' she said, 'for being honest.'

So why did he feel like the biggest bastard in the universe?

'I'm sorry,' he said again. And, because the emotional stuff was getting too much for him and he needed to escape, he added, 'I'd better go and get Truffle.'

Georgie stayed curled in bed until she heard the front door close.

Ryan McGregor was strong, silent, stubborn—and oh, so stupid.

Why did he have to be so difficult about this?

Why couldn't he take that leap of faith and just *try* to see where things went between them?

It seemed that friendship was the most he was going to offer. Take it or leave it.

He'd been honest with her, unlike Charlie. Ryan hadn't lied to her, and she knew he would never cheat. But she was also pretty sure he wouldn't budge. He wasn't going to give them a chance. And that hurt so, so much.

What was so wrong with her that he didn't feel comfortable taking a risk with her? Was she right about there being something lacking in her—the same thing Charlie had obviously picked up on when he'd turned to Trisha?

And how were they going to deal with the rest of the job swap?

He'd asked her to stay. But not because he wanted her: because, she thought, he felt guilty about letting Clara down.

Perhaps she'd been right in the first place to think about finding somewhere else to stay. Though asking someone at the hospital where she could find somewhere else to live—that would make it obvious there were problems between herself and Ryan. And everyone would jump to conclusions and gossip, and once the truth was out everyone would start to pity her—the very thing she'd tried so hard to avoid in London.

What an idiot she'd been.

She should've said no last night. Gone to bed on her own, instead of giving in to the temptation to make love with him. It would still have been awkward between them for a while, but at least the situation would've been salvageable. Whereas now she knew what it felt like to make love with him and fall asleep in his arms. She'd lied to herself that it was just for comfort, just for fun, that her heart wasn't involved.

But her heart was involved. Somewhere along the way, she'd fallen in love with the dour Scot who was great with his colleagues and his patients, but who kept a huge barrier between himself and the rest of the world because he was too scared to let himself get close to someone again and be let down. A man who trusted his dog and his best friend, and steadfastly refused to open his heart to anyone else.

If she'd been enough for him, then he would've taken the risk and let down his barriers.

But she wasn't.

She hadn't been enough for Charlie—the man she'd married but who'd made a baby with someone else, instead of her—and she wasn't enough for Ryan.

And the rest of the job swap was going to be the same nightmare she'd tried to leave behind in London: where she'd be lying to everyone, saying that everything was absolutely fine, when in reality her heart was a wreck.

She'd get through it. There was no other choice.

But she was never, ever going to let herself fall for anyone again.

CHAPTER NINE

RYAN AND GEORGIE spent the next few days being super-polite to each other, careful to keep the topic of conversations to work and Truffle. At work, it was easy to focus on their patients and their colleagues, deflecting conversation away from their feelings, but at the cottage it was more and more awkward. Apart from sharing meals and chores, Georgie spent most of her time at the cottage curled on her bed with a book.

And it was horrible.

She missed the old easiness between them. She missed cuddling up on the sofa with Truffle. She missed the way Ryan teased her about trying everything Scottish.

It was starting to be a struggle at work, too, and she was terrified that one of their colleagues would notice that things were strained between them. She was just glad that the situation with Truffle meant they'd already moved their shifts round so they were on opposites for as much as possible.

But she was glad of Ryan's arrival when she called for the crash team on the day when she was on an early and he was on a late.

She was performing chest compressions on a ten-month-old who'd stopped breathing in the middle of tests, pushing down on the little girl's breastbone with the tips of two fingers, then giving two breaths after fifteen compressions, her mouth sealing the infant's nose and mouth.

He grabbed a mask and bag. 'I'll compress, you bag,' he said.

After a minute, he asked, 'Any cough or gag response?'

'No.'

'OK.' He checked the brachial pulse. 'Nothing. We'll keep going.'

It took them another ten minutes of chest compressions and breathing via the mask and bag, but finally the little girl responded.

'Let's get her on a ventilator,' Ryan said. 'And then we'll talk to her parents. Run me through the case.'

'Mollie's ten months old. She had an unsettled night, and her mum took her to the family doctor, who said it was just mucus. Then she got hiccups and was struggling to breathe, and the doctor told her mum to bring her here.

I'd put her on oxygen, inserted a cannula and taken a blood test, but then she crashed on me. The rest of it you know.'

'OK. You did all the right things,' he said.

Once Mollie was on the ventilator, Georgie introduced Ryan to Mollie's mum.

'What's happening?' Mollie's mum bit her lip. 'Today's been a nightmare. Mollie had that shocking cold and the doctor said it was just mucus, but then she started hiccupping and she couldn't get her breath. I called the doctor...' She shuddered. 'Thank God my neighbour was home and could drive me here with her. And then the nurse asked me to come out of the room. Is Mollie going to—going to—?' Her face crumpled as she clearly couldn't bring herself to voice her worst fears.

'That's why we're here to update you,' Georgie said gently. 'Mollie's heart stopped, which was why the nurse asked you to come away—it's really not very nice for parents to see, but please don't worry because I'm glad to say we got her heart started again.'

Mollie's mum had a hand across her mouth in horror. 'Her heart *stopped*? Oh, my God. Is she going to be all right?'

'We hope so,' Ryan said, 'But at the moment we need to keep her sedated and cooled down, to make sure her brain doesn't start swelling.

We've got her on a ventilator, which makes sure she breathes properly, and we're keeping a very close eye on her.'

'A ventilator?' Mollie's mum gasped, her eyes widening in horror. 'She's sedated? So she—you're keeping her asleep?'

Georgie squeezed her hand. 'It sounds scary, and it looks scary, but it's the best way to keep her safe right now. In a couple of days, we'll wake her up and see how she manages or if she needs further support.'

'My baby.' Mollie's mum was clearly having trouble processing what had happened. 'Can I see her?'

'Of course,' Ryan said. 'Because we've sedated her, I need to warn you now that she won't respond to you the way she normally does, but she'll still be able to hear you if you sit and talk to her, and she'll definitely know if you're holding her hand.'

'Can we call anyone for you?' Georgie asked. 'Mollie's dad?'

'I… He's away working on the rigs. He'll be devastated.'

'We're happy to talk to him if you need us to,' Georgie said. 'Is there another relative or friend who could come and be with you? Your neighbour?'

'No—he had to go to work after he dropped

us here.' Mollie's mum looked anguished. 'I'll call my husband but I don't know when he'll be able to get here.' She shook her head as if to clear it. 'Everyone's at work or they're miles away and won't be able to get here for ages.'

'I'm due off duty shortly,' Georgie said, 'so I'll stay and sit with you until someone can join you.'

'But you've been at work all day.'

'I'll sit with you. Come on. I'll make you a cup of tea, and introduce you to the nurses in the intensive care unit, and keep you company for a bit. I'll sit with Mollie while you call her dad and whoever else you need to call.'

'That's—that's so good of you. You're a kind lass,' Mollie's mum said.

'And I'm due a break around tea-time,' Ryan said, 'so I'll come and have my mug of coffee with you, too. And you can ask us anything you want and we'll do our best to answer.'

Mollie's mum looked close to tears. 'Mollie's our only one, and we had three rounds of IVF to get her. If anything happens to her...'

'It's much too early to start worrying about that,' Georgie said, giving her a hug. 'And your Mollie's a fighter. We got her back after her heart stopped, so let's take it one day at a time for now.'

* * *

Mollie was still touch and go the next day, but her father had flown in from the oil rig to be there with his wife and baby. On her breaks, Georgie went in to see them with coffee and sandwiches.

'Thank you, that's kind of you, but I can't face anything,' Mollie's mum said.

'I know you're worried sick,' Georgie said, 'but you need to keep your strength up. Both of you. You'll be no good to Mollie if you keel over, will you? *Eat.*'

Though there was a nasty moment later in her shift in the ward round, when Georgie was checking Mollie's obs and the little girl's heart rate started dropping; thankfully, by the time she'd grabbed Ryan to come and help, Mollie's heart rate had gone back to where it should be.

'Sorry. I wasted your time,' she mumbled when they left the room.

'No, you did the right thing,' he said. 'Is there anything else?'

Yes. I want you to stop being so ridiculously stubborn and give us a chance.

But she knew it was pointless even trying, and she wasn't going to let him reject her again. 'I don't think so,' she said coolly, and went back to doing her ward round.

* * *

Normally, Ryan didn't take his work home with him.

But he couldn't stop thinking about little Mollie. The terror in her mum's eyes when she'd realised how serious the situation was. The way Georgie had been so calm and so kind, patiently going over things again whenever either of Mollie's parents asked her to explain something.

And it wasn't just being a good doctor. Georgie, he thought, would make a great mum. He'd watched her on the ward with their sick patients, and she seemed to have a knack for knowing just when a little one wanted a cuddle or a story. She made time to do it, too, even if it meant she missed a break or had to eat her lunch while she was catching up with paperwork.

Georgie would be at the heart of any family she made.

She was good with Truffle, too. Even though she'd had little contact with dogs before coming to Scotland, she'd made an effort with his Labrador, learning how to play games to distract the dog and tire her out while she was on enforced rest. Just as she'd be with a fractious child.

'You treat her the way that other men would

treat their child. You've told me yourself that she's your family...'

Her words to him, that awful morning, came back to haunt him.

Did he treat his dog as if she was his child?

And did it follow that maybe, just maybe, he might know how to be a dad?

'You're putting all these barriers in the way, but they're not as big as you think they are.'

Was she right about that, too? Was he worrying too much? Could he overcome his resistance and just let himself be loved, be part of a family?

Every time he'd tried it, it had gone wrong. And he knew he was at fault, because he couldn't let people close.

But was Georgie right in that all he had to do was reach out? Was it really that simple?

Did he want a family?

This felt like picking a scab. Sore, stupid and a waste of time. He had to stop thinking about it, he told himself.

Except he couldn't.

He kept wondering. Did he want a family? Did he want a family with Georgina Jones?

He was beginning to think the answer was yes.

And he needed to find the right time to tell her. Reach out. Ask her to be his.

* * *

Two days later, Ryan reviewed Mollie's obs. 'I think we can try taking her off sedation today,' he said. 'If I'm not happy with the way she reacts, I'll put her back on sedation for another day or so, but let's give this a try.'

Georgie joined him for the procedure and checked that Mollie was managing to breathe adequately on her own; and between them they monitored her while she woke.

Had there been too much damage before she'd gone on the ventilator, or had she turned a corner? Ryan's heart was in his mouth. After Truffle had gone missing, he had a much better idea of how hard situations like this were for parents.

Yeah. He knew now that Georgie was right about that. For him, Truffle was just like the child he'd refused to make with Zoe. He'd worried himself as sick over a simple operation as Mollie's parents had over something much more complicated.

Like it or not, he was a dad. Of sorts.

Finally, the baby opened her eyes.

'Talk to her,' he said to Mollie's mum.

'Mollie? It's Mama,' she whispered, her voice thick with tears.

When the little girl smiled, Ryan felt tears

of mingled relief and joy pricking his own eyelids. He looked over at Georgie and saw that her eyes were glistening with unshed tears, too.

He knew there was still a way to go, but it looked as if Mollie was going to make it.

If only, he thought, he and Georgie could make it. Because seeing the love between Mollie's parents, seeing how they'd supported each other in a crisis and watched over their precious, desperately wanted child…it had made him think. Made him *want*. Made him think that maybe he'd been wrong to keep that distance between himself and Georgie, that maybe he should've given them both a chance.

She'd be an amazing mum. And maybe she could teach him to be a good dad. A good partner.

Could he let Georgie close, the way he hadn't been able to let Zoe close?

But she was so professional with him, at Hayloft Cottage as well as at work. She kept her distance. How, then, could he find the right words to tell her that he'd changed his mind, that he'd made a mistake and wanted to try things her way?

Maybe he needed to make a huge gesture. Hire a skywriter to say, *Forgive me, I was wrong, I want to make a go of it.*

He wanted to tell her. He just didn't know how. And the thoughts just kept spinning in his head.

Mollie progressed so well during the next week that she was able to go home. Georgie had just finished the discharge process when she realised that she was feeling odd. There was a weird metallic taste in her mouth. Was she going down with some kind of virus?

She shrugged it off, but a bit later on she noticed that her breasts were feeling tender.

It took the rest of her shift to realise that, actually, there might be a different reason for feeling that way. Her periods were regular almost to the hour, and she was late.

She took a deep breath. How ridiculous. Of course she wasn't pregnant. She and Ryan had used a condom.

But the only completely reliable contraception was abstinence. And a teeny, tiny proportion of condoms failed.

Telling herself that she was being utterly ridiculous, she drove home via a supermarket she didn't normally use. Thankfully she couldn't see anyone she knew in the aisles, but even so she hid the pregnancy test in her basket underneath a magazine.

Ryan was on a late, so she had time to do the

test, reassure herself that everything was fine, and get rid of the evidence.

Once she'd made a fuss of Truffle, she went up to the bathroom and did the test.

Of course it was going to be negative. She'd bought the sort that would give you a result even before you'd officially missed a period, just for that extra layer of reassurance.

She washed her hands, then stood and watched the screen on the pregnancy test; the hourglass flashed to show that the test was working.

According to the instructions, it would take up to three minutes to see the result.

It felt like the longest three minutes of her life. Every time she checked her watch, only a few seconds had passed.

And then, finally, the words came up on the screen: but not the ones she had hoped for.

The black, bold type told her the truth very clearly.

Pregnant 1-2 weeks

She went cold. Ryan, who was absolutely adamant that he didn't want children.

What was she going to do?

She'd wanted a baby with her husband, a man who hadn't wanted a family with her but had made a baby with his mistress. And now she was accidentally pregnant by a man who'd told her all along that he didn't want children.

There were no guarantees that she'd carry this baby to term. She had a twenty-five per cent chance of having a miscarriage. Or she could choose to terminate the pregnancy.

She wrapped her arms around herself. Now she knew she was pregnant, the yearnings she'd suppressed were back in full force. So maybe this baby wasn't a disaster: maybe this baby was a gift.

From Joshua's experience, she knew that being a single parent wasn't an easy option. But she also knew that her family and friends would support her. She wouldn't be alone.

But she would have to tell Ryan. She was barely halfway through the job swap, and there was no way she could keep her pregnancy a secret. She'd be showing by the time the swap came to an end. It would be obvious to everyone.

How was he going to react to the news? He was a good man, a man with integrity, so she knew his first instinct would be to support her. But he'd said he didn't want children. So would he walk away from her and be a father in name only, or would he give them a chance? Would he give himself a chance to be part of a family, something he hadn't had for thirty years?

Numbly, she went downstairs. Truffle pushed her nose into Georgie's hand, as if to comfort her.

'He's not going to be happy about this,' Georgie said softly. 'Not happy at all.'

Truffle moved closer.

'How am I going to tell him?'

Truffle gave a soft wuff, which made Georgie smile but also made her sad. Because there wasn't an answer. She didn't have a clue how to tell him.

She thought about it as she made chicken and apple stew for dinner.

She thought about it a bit more as she baked some brownies, on the grounds that the scent of vanilla and chocolate helped to relax her.

But she still hadn't come up with an answer by the time Ryan walked in.

'Hi.' Georgie took a deep breath. 'I made stew.'

'Thanks, but I'm not hungry.'

Meaning he'd had a rough day? Well, she was about to make it even rougher. 'I think you should eat.'

He frowned. 'Why?'

'Because we need to talk.'

He looked at her. 'You're moving out?'

Very probably, after what she was going to tell him. She said nothing, but heated the stew through on the hob and put some rice in the microwave.

Ryan didn't make it easy for her, either. He ate in complete silence. Well, he ate half of it, probably because he didn't want to be rude, she thought.

He pushed his plate away. 'So what did you want to talk about?'

'There isn't a nice way to say this,' she said, 'so I'll tell you straight. But, first, I want you to know that I don't expect anything from you.'

He frowned. 'You're not making much sense.'

Tell him.

'The night of the ceilidh.' She swallowed hard. 'There were consequences.'

She watched the colour drain from his face as he absorbed her news. 'But we used a condom.'

'You're a medic. You know as well as I do that the only absolutely certain method of contraception is abstinence. Yes, the chances making a baby when you use a condom are tiny, but they exist. And we made a baby.'

Ryan stared at Georgie, utterly shocked.

Had she just said…?

'We made a baby?' he echoed, knowing he

sounded utterly stupid, but he couldn't get his head around this. The words felt like some kind of white noise in his head, making no sense.

She inclined her head.

Pregnant. With his baby.

'When did you find out?'

'Today. After my shift. I've had a couple of hours to think about it. And to talk to Truffle.'

'She's a good listener.'

'She's not so great on the advice, though. Her answer to everything is "woof".'

Ryan knew that Georgie was trying to lighten the mood, but he could see the tears glimmering in her eyes. One slid over the edge of her lashes and trickled down her cheek. Before she could scrub it away, he reached out and wiped it away gently with the pad of his thumb.

'Say something,' she said.

He didn't know what to say. Her news had fried his brain. 'What do you want to do?' he asked.

'I didn't try to trap you into getting me pregnant—' she began.

'They were my condoms and it was my responsibility,' he cut in, 'so of course you didn't get pregnant on purpose. If anything, it was my fault.'

She shook her head. 'It takes two to make a baby.'

He was pretty sure he knew the answer, but he asked anyway. Just to be clear. 'Do you want to keep it?'

She nodded. 'As I said, I don't expect anything from you. I know my parents will be supportive, my brother will be supportive and my niece will love the idea of having a cousin.'

Her parents. Her brother. Her niece. He worked it out. 'So you're going back to London and having the baby there?'

'That,' she said, 'depends on you.'

'How?'

'What do you want?'

'I...' All the way along, he'd told her that he didn't want children. He'd been starting to think that maybe he'd been wrong, particularly when he'd seen her with little Mollie and thought about what Georgie had told him about the way he treated Truffle. And now she'd just told him she was expecting his child.

He was going to be a dad.

There was a tight ball in his chest. 'You know my marriage broke up because I didn't want children and Zoe did.'

She was silent, as if working out what his words meant for her. 'Supposing Zoe had fallen pregnant accidentally—what would you have done?' she asked. 'Would you have insisted that she have a termination? Or would you have walked out on her?'

What kind of man did she think he was? 'No, of course not. I would've stood by her.' He looked at her. 'So there's your answer. I'll stand by you. I'll support the child—and you—financially.'

'What about emotionally?'

And that was the rub. 'I don't do emotions.' Well, he did; but he didn't know how to do them the way other people wanted them.

'Oh, but you do,' she said. 'When Truffle went missing, you were devastated. You love that dog.'

'We're not discussing Truffle.'

'Yes, we are. I've said before, you love that dog as if she were a child.'

He'd come to realise that, thanks to her. 'All right,' he conceded. 'I love my dog.'

'And she loves you,' she continued, utterly remorseless. 'Look at her now—she can see you're worried and upset, and she's right by your side.'

And she was. Truffle was sitting as close to him as she could possibly get, leaning against him, with her chin on her knee as if to say that she was there and she'd never desert him.

'So you *do* do emotions. Truffle's the walking proof of that.'

Where was she taking this? 'I guess,' he said guardedly.

'But I think you use her to deflect your human feelings.'

That was probably also true. But he didn't know what to say.

'And you told me you loved Zoe.'

'I did.'

'So,' she said. 'Maybe you could learn to love our child.'

And he could see in her eyes the thing she didn't dare to say. *Maybe you could learn to love me.*

He thought about it. When Truffle had gone missing, Georgie had been there by his side and helped him find the dog. She'd been there by his side at the vet's. She'd listened to him, and she had still been there by his side afterwards to help him look after Truffle.

At work, last week, she'd sat with Mollie's mum when it was above and beyond the call of duty. She'd refused to leave the poor woman to wait alone until a family member or friend could come to support her. And he'd seen Georgie do that with other anxious parents too, over the last three months.

So it followed that she wouldn't abandon him or their child.

He could trust her.

And he liked the way he felt when he was with her. He liked the way she made him see things differently.

Could he see a baby differently? A baby of his own? The baby he'd always told himself he didn't want—but, if he was honest with himself, the baby he thought he didn't deserve because he wasn't lovable enough?

He'd told himself that he didn't know how to be a father. But Georgie seemed to believe he could do it.

He thought about it some more. What about the practicalities? Would she expect him to move back to London with her? Truffle would hate that and so would he; he'd feel hemmed in, in the city. But would she be prepared to stay here with him?

There was only one way to find out.

Ask her.

He'd never, ever felt this nervous and unsure before. He'd never told anyone the deepest, darkest secret of his heart. Maybe it was time to be totally honest.

'What if I fail? What if I'm a rubbish dad and a rubbish partner and I let you down?'

Hope bloomed in her eyes. 'I don't think you'll fail. I'm not looking for perfection, and neither is our baby. Just for someone who'll love us all the way back.' She reached out and took his hand. 'And you won't let us down. Just keep being you. A bit less of the silent and stubborn would be helpful, but I don't want to change you.' She took a deep breath.

'So I'll take the risk and say it. I love you, Ryan McGregor. Even if you were Grumpy Mc-Grumpface when I first met you. I love everything about you. The way you notice things and sort things out quietly and without a fuss. The way you insist on seeing everything rationally, yet you can still see the magic in the Northern Lights—and the way you kissed me under them made me weak at the knees. I think that's when I started to fall in love with you. And the night you danced with me at the ceilidh—that was when I realised I wanted you. For keeps.'

She loved him.

'And, just so you know,' she said, 'I wasn't necessarily planning to go back to London. Actually, if you turn me down, I'm going to camp on your doorstep until you agree to let me into your life. The way I see it, you and Truffle are mine, just as the baby and I are yours.'

Camp on his doorstep?

Those were the words of a woman who wasn't going to abandon him. A woman whose family and half her friends would be four hundred miles away if she stayed here in Edinburgh, but she wanted him—loved him—enough to make that distance work.

'So I'm yours, then,' he said.

'Uh-huh.'

'Ryan Jones,' he said, testing out the name.

She shook her head. 'That's Charlie's surname. If you really want to take mine, you'd be Ryan Woodhouse.' She looked at him. 'Though if we're talking name changes, I think Georgina McGregor has a nice ring to it. All those Gs, softie southerner first name and tough Scots last name. That's us all over.'

Only Georgie could have come up with that.

And it felt as if the barriers round his heart, the ones he'd thought were impenetrable, were dissolving. Melted away by the deepest of emotions: love.

'Are you asking me to marry you?'

'If that's what it takes, sure. I'll drop down on my knee and propose. Though a piece of paper isn't going to make the slightest bit of difference to the way I feel.' Her face lit up as she looked at him. 'You're not Charlie—you're not going to be careless with me. You're stubborn, but I think you love me too and you just don't know how to say it.'

How could she see inside his head like that?

'So I'm happy to be the one to say it first. I love you, Ryan McGregor, and I want you to be my family.' She nudged the dog. 'Your turn to speak. Tell him you want to be a family with me and the baby, too.'

'Woof,' Truffle said obligingly.

A baby. A family. A woman who really, really loved him.

Things he'd never thought to have.

He remembered what she'd said to him before. *'All you have to do is reach out.'*

He'd told himself it was too hard; but it wasn't. What was hard was trusting that it would be easy. But he trusted Georgie. The calm, capable, professional doctor who put his head in a spin and put fire in his heart. The one who'd shown him that the world was a kinder, warmer place than he'd thought it was.

All he had to do was reach out.

'I'm traditional,' he said. 'So I'll be the one to do the asking.' He dropped down on one knee and took her hand. 'You barrelled into my life on a horrendous day, and you brought the sunshine with you even though it was stoating. Since I've met you, I've seen the world with different eyes and I might even think now the Loch Ness Monster is possible. You taught me to wish on a falling star. I made one wish with you—a wish that came true—so I'm hoping the second one I made will come true, too.' He dragged in a breath.

'A wish I barely admitted even to myself. I don't remember what it's like to be part of a family because it was so long ago. But I do know my mum would've adored you as much as I do. And I want a family. A family of my own. A family of you and our baby. You've a heart the size of the world, Georgie, and you make the world a better place. You make *my* world a better place. I love you. Will you marry me, Georgina Jones, be my love for the rest of our days? You, and our baby?'

She leaned down to kiss him. 'Yes. I'd be honoured. I'm absolutely not going to promise to obey you,' she warned, 'but I'll love you, I'll honour you and I'll cherish you until the end of my days. I don't care where or when we get married, and we have plenty of time to sort out where we live. I'm thinking anywhere that has a decent-sized garden for Truffle and the baby and incredibly good fences Truffle can't dig under.' She coughed. 'But there is one thing that's less negotiable.'

'One thing? What's that?' He held his breath. What did she want?

Her face went pink. 'I'd rather like you to marry me in a kilt. The one you wore the night we made our baby.'

The heat in her expression made his blood sizzle. 'I think I can manage that.' He paused and gave her a look that he hoped made her blood sizzle, too. 'Provided you take it off me on our wedding night.'

'That's guaranteed,' she said. 'But those buckles looked a bit tricky. I might need some practice.'

'Just as I need some practice in telling you I love you,' he said. 'I think lessons should start now, Dr McGregor-to-be. I love you.'

'I love you, too.'

'Good. Let's make a start on those buckles,' he said, getting to his feet and scooping her up.

'Hang on. I thought you said carrying me up the spiral staircase was a bad idea?' she said as he strode towards the middle of the room.

'That was then. Now you're my family—and I know I'm not going to drop you, because you believe in me. With you, I'm not going to fail at anything. You're my world, Georgie, and I love you.' He kissed her. 'I really, really love you.'

She kissed him back. 'For now and for always.'

* * * * *

*Look out for the next story in the
Changing Shifts duet*

Family for the Children's Doc
by Scarlet Wilson

*And if you enjoyed this story, check out
these other great reads from
Kate Hardy*

Mistletoe Proposal on the Children's Ward
A Nurse and a Pup to Heal Him
Heart Surgeon, Prince…Husband!
Carrying the Single Dad's Baby

All available now!